SAM CRESCENT

EVERNIGHT PUBLISHING ®

www.evernightpublishing.com

ZERO

Copyright© 2018

Sam Crescent

Editor: Karyn White

Cover Artist: Sour Cherry Designs

Jacket Design: Jay Aheer

ISBN: 978-1-77339-668-2

SAM CRESCENT

DEDICATION

The Skulls mean a great deal to me and I want to thank Evernight and all the team who bring these books to life. Without you all *The Skulls* wouldn't have a home.

Thank you to my readers. Your support and kindness means the world to me.

SAM CRESCENT

ZERO

The Skulls, 6

Sam Crescent

Copyright © 2014

Prologue

Ten years ago

Lucas Blakely flicked his cigarette onto the pavement before exhaling the last puff of smoke into the air. Life was good. Life was fucking good. Becoming part of The Skulls was the best decision he ever made. They were all a family, and even though he was a prospect, getting all the shitty jobs, he didn't care at all. He'd rather be shoveling shit for the club than doing anything else with his life. Zero knew how bad life could be without the club, and he wasn't going to do anything to turn it to shit. For the first time in his life he felt like he finally belonged. His parents didn't give a shit about him, and neither did any of the family in his life. The only real family he had besides the club was Prudence and Trevor. Prudence, however, always went by the name Prue. He'd do anything for the brother and sister pair. Thinking about his two friends, he wondered what Trevor had gotten himself into. His friend wasn't known for making good decisions, but Lucas wouldn't worry.

Trevor wouldn't do anything stupid to put Prue in danger. The one thing Lucas could guarantee was Prue's protection. He cared about her more than any other woman in his life. She deserved true happiness after everything she'd gone through.

Relaxing, Lucas stared up at the night sky feeling calm, relaxed, and alive. He wasn't going to leave The Skulls. Getting his patch was going to be the best thing he ever achieved in his life. He dropped out of school at a young age without a single certificate to his name. Tiny made sure he achieved a mechanic's certificate, giving him the excuse to work on cars in his free time. All of the men he met were qualified to work on the machines.

With The Skulls he could be himself without any worry. They accepted him for who he was rather than what they expected.

Feminine giggling caught his attention, and he saw Lash and Nash messing around. The two men already had their club names while he had to wait for his. They were also prospects and working to be patched in. Tiny was a fair leader and never showed favoritism even with the two brothers living with him. Running a hand over his face, Lucas threw the cigarette away and started back inside. His cell phone rang, and he pulled it out accepting the call.

"Lucas?" Trevor asked, sounding terrified.

Frowning, he looked around the grounds, not seeing anything suspicious.

"Trevor, what's up?"

They hadn't seen each other in over two months. The last time they were together they had spent the weekend drunk off their faces. He recalled Prue cursing and cleaning up the mess they'd created.

"I've fucked up, man. Shit, I need your help. I'm so fucking fucked."

Lucas heard the nerves in his friend's voice. Feeling his gut clench, he glanced down at the time. It was past ten on a Friday. The club was roaring with life. Men were fucking and drinking, the action finally starting to get good.

"Where are you?" Lucas asked.

"I'm in a hotel outside of Fort Wills. The, erm, fuck, er, it's called The Central Point, whatever the fuck that means. I need your help. Fuck, it hurts," Trevor whimpered over the line. The panic was clear to Lucas.

"It doesn't matter what it's called. Just stay put. I know where you are. I'll be there soon. Don't go anywhere."

He pocketed his phone, grabbed his bike, and drove out of the compound. Lucas tried to think about what was going on with his friend. What had Trevor gotten himself into? Lucas didn't want to think about it, but he knew it was bad.

Lucas climbed off his bike seeing the name of the hotel was the same that Trevor said.

One of the doors in the corner opened, and Lucas paused as he saw his friend. Trevor was usually so full of life, running everywhere. No one could stop him or hold him down. Staring at his friend, Lucas saw him holding his stomach. Even in the dim lighting he spotted the blood and the paleness on his face.

Panicking, he ran to Trevor's side.

"Fuck, what are you doing? You should be in the hospital." He pulled his cell phone out ready to call for an ambulance.

Trevor stopped him. "No, no hospital. If I go then Prue doesn't stand a chance."

"What? What the fuck is going on?" They were on the ground outside of Trevor's room. Tears filled Lucas's eyes as he looked down at his friend. The fucker was dying in his arms, and Lucas couldn't let that happen. They were best friends. He needed to save him. They had been together forever, and Lucas intended to get him patched in with The Skulls.

"I fucked up." Trevor gasped, groaning.

"Stop talking."

"No! No hospital. I'm not going to the hospital. They'll kill me, and then they'll be after Prue. I can't do that to her. She deserves so much better. Fuck!"

Lucas lifted up the shirt and gasped. There was no saving the man in his arms. No, he couldn't let his best friend die. This shit was not happening.

"Who did this?"

"I thought I could handle it. The money was good. Fuck!" Trevor was wheezing, and there was a pause after each word.

The tears in Lucas's eyes fell thick and fast. "Don't die. Let me take you to the hospital."

"I'm a dead man, Lucas. I worked for Alan, Alan Lynch. He's ... he's a man I never want Prue to meet. He makes your biker gang look like kids' play." Trevor coughed. "He's a type of mafia man. Drugs, guns, girls, money, he does everything. I worked for him. I took some drugs to a rival. Fuck, I was stitched up, Lucas. I was stitched up bad."

He listened to his friend knowing it was only a matter of minutes before Trevor died.

"He takes out all the loved ones. I need you to promise me you'll keep Prue safe. She doesn't know anything about this. I kept it from her because I'm a fucking idiot." Trevor cried out. "Promise me."

"I promise. I'll do everything to keep her safe."

Trevor smiled, and his whole body started to shake. "End this, man. I can't handle it, please. With Prue take care of, I don't need this shit. I fucked up."

Lucas watched as Trevor reached into his pocket. "Take this. Read it when you get the chance."

Taking the letter off his friend, Lucas couldn't stop the tears falling thick and fast. His best friend had asked him to end his life. Why hadn't he checked in sooner with Trevor? He should have known something had gone wrong. Closing his eyes, Lucas covered Trevor's mouth, stopping the air. Though his friend fought, within minutes he was dead in his arms, the fight gone completely out of him.

Pocketing the letter, Lucas stared at the man in his arms. His best friend was dead, and the man responsible was Alan Lynch. He'd never heard of the man before. Wiping the tears from his face with the hand not covered in blood, he looked around him. Fuck, he didn't know if there were any witnesses.

"Prue."

Dumping the body in the hotel room, he climbed on his bike and rode for Prue. He knew some guys who'd keep her protected. Trevor wouldn't lie about her protection. She would need to disappear. Tears fell down his face, but he ignored them. There was no time to cry or think about his dead friend. Fuck, Trevor was dead.

The time passed quickly as he made his way toward Prue and Trevor's house. When he saw the light on in her bedroom, he parked the bike. What was he supposed to do? Protect Prue, and then deal with everything else. A dead body left in a hotel room was going to get way too much attention.

You can do this.

Getting to the porch he found the key hidden in the plant pot. Many years he'd known the two and they still hid a spare key in the plant pot. Letting himself inside, he called out Prue's name. Should he get The Skulls involved? They'd know what to do. The moment the thought occurred, he rejected it. He was a prospect, and he didn't want to bring this kind of shit to them. Within minutes she appeared at the top of the stairs looking ruffled.

"Lucas, what the fuck?" she asked, rubbing at her eyes. She wasn't wearing her glasses and was clearly struggling to see. Prue had been wearing glasses for as long as he could remember. "What are you doing here?"

"You've got to get dressed and pack your shit up. We need to move. I don't know how long we've got before they come," he said, going into the kitchen. Trevor hadn't been particularly clear on how long he had to get her safe. Lucas didn't want to waste unnecessary time.

"Leave, Lucas, what the fuck?" She repeated her words making her way down to him.

"Trevor is dead," he said, forcing the words out between gritted teeth. "He's in serious trouble. You didn't fucking tell me he was in serious trouble."

"He said he was fine. Shit. I knew I should have asked him more. He was always so quiet, and he wouldn't bring anyone back to the house." Prue ran fingers through her hair. She was nineteen years old. Their parents had died in a fatal shooting when she was fifteen. None of them lived near Fort Wills at the time, and it was only a year ago when Trevor had got this house for her to live in, finally moving them out of their parents' old place. Trevor had taken responsibility for her, and Zero helped bring her up since she was fifteen. Neither of them would let her go into care.

"You need to leave," he said.

"Who was he working for? He wouldn't tell me, but I know he'd tell you."

Should he tell her? What harm would it really do? Trevor had already put her in more danger.

"Alan Lynch."

She gasped, putting a hand to her mouth. "No, he wouldn't. How the fuck could he do something like that?"

"He worked for him and got killed for it. I need you to move." Once Alan's name was mentioned, Lucas didn't need to fight her to move her ass. Prue packed up everything she needed, taking birth certificates and the necessary documents. When she was packed and on the back of his bike, he rode to a safe house he knew. The city was perfect for getting rid of folk who needed to disappear. With his focus on keeping Prue safe, he could stop thinking about the pain of losing his best friend.

Lucas bundled her away with an old friend who specialized in fake identities. He knew a lot of people to help him. It was one of the reasons why Butch was securing him a position at The Skulls. They could use him to help them.

He organized for Prue to disappear and that he'd come for her when he was ready. She didn't want him to go, but he had no choice. He wasn't finished with his own kind of business. Leaving her alone, he went back to the hotel where Trevor was lying, decaying, dead. Nothing would bring him back. His best friend was dead, never coming back to drink with him. *No, I can't allow that to happen, but it's too late, and there's nothing I can do.* Alan Lynch had guaranteed that. Trevor was gone.

Staring at him on the bed, Lucas couldn't think of a single thing to say to his one true friend. The pain engulfed him, threatening to tear him in two. He let the tears fall not caring how weak it made him feel. His best friend was dead. The words kept ringing through his head, and he couldn't believe it. An hour later, his cell phone rang.

"Where the fuck are you?" Butch asked.

"I've got stuff to do."

"What do you mean you've got stuff to do? Your life is the club. Lash and Nash are picking up the fucking slack. Get your ass back here."

Lucas was silent as he listened to his other friend berate him. "Butch, can I ask you something?"

"Sure. I've got all fucking day for questions. Why not fire them at me?"

Staring at Trevor, he felt the will to do something that would get him killed. "If someone you cared about was killed, what would you do?"

"I'd kill the bastard dead, Lucas. No one fucks with me and gets away with it, and that means you. I've not been patched in that long, but the way you're going you're going to get me fucking killed," Butch said.

"You'd kill them?"

"Yes, no one fucks with me."

Lucas knew what he had to do. "There's something I've got to do this weekend. I'll be back on Monday."

Hanging up the phone, he looked at Trevor. The only thing he could do was get rid of the body. He went to the gas station and loaded up a can. Inside Trevor's room, he poured the petrol all over the body and across the hotel room. Striking the match, he left the room to burn, getting on his bike to make his way to the city.

****

For the last twenty-four hours, Lucas had watched and gathered as much information as possible from everyone who hated Alan Lynch. Considering the man's power, he didn't have anyone who wanted to stick by his side. Most of the people Lucas spoke to were more than happy to give shit up for the man. Lucas knew Alan would be visiting his club, Pleasures, tonight. Pleasures was where he was going to get the man he needed.

Leaving his bike and leather cut in a secure holding, he rented out a van.

Lucas made all the arrangements to guarantee he'd get what he needed. The letter in his jacket still lay there unopened. Trevor had written him a letter, his last words. Lucas wasn't ready to read them yet. First, he needed to get a little payback.

You're not going to make it out alive.

He was going to take Alan out, and if he went down with him, he'd be happy. Lucas didn't care if he made it out alive, as long as he hurt Alan in the process. Going unnoticed, he followed Alan to the club seeing his entourage of security men. From the age of ten, Lucas had been learning how to fire a gun. He learned with Trevor, and by fifteen he was an expert shooter.

At twenty-three years old he was a machine, deadly. He could hold his own in The Skulls. It was the only place he wanted to be. Rubbing a hand down his face, he carried the weapons in the back of his jeans. There was no metal security detector on the way inside the club. He entered the bar and ordered himself a beer. Looking around the tight space he saw the women, the drugs, and settled his gaze on Alan. The man was in a VIP section, which was partitioned off with glass. The moment Alan stood, he'd be easy to kill.

Was this some kind of power trip to show everyone else how powerful he was?

Alan fucked with the wrong man.

Sipping at his beer, he checked the security of the men. They were bored and used to working like this to keep him safe. The men were not even on their guard. Didn't they expect anyone to try to take out their boss? Once he started shooting, he would have to work quickly to get out of there.

He killed Trevor. No walking away, no backing

out.

Fight to the death.

He and Trevor had promised each other a lifetime of friendship. Nothing could keep either of them from what they wanted—until this fucker had taken Trevor away from him.

Kill him. Hurt him.

Trevor died slowly. The only person he'd called was Lucas.

Waiting for the right opportunity was his best course of action. Sipping at his beer, he saw the right opportunity as Alan's security guards turned their backs on the crowd, bored with looking after someone who wasn't in danger.

They were mistaken. Getting closer was easier. Lucas had learned to fire both guns at the same time. The summers growing up he's spent the time practicing to fire both as he wanted to be like the cowboys in the movies. Not many men could fire two guns at the same time, but he'd trained to the point of ease.

Drawing them out, he took out the first two men along with the three charging toward them. With them down, he ran toward the glass, knocked Alan out and dragged him out of the back of the club. He had learned the layout of the club easily. Adrenaline pumping through his veins, Lucas continued to move, all the time thinking about his best friend.

He dumped Alan in the back of his truck he'd rented and drove to the abandoned glass building he found in the outskirt of the city. The windows were smashed, and there were cobwebs everywhere. Securing Alan to the chair took little effort. Lucas stared at the man who had taken Trevor away from him and Prue. His morbid thoughts were starting to sound like a broken record.

The man was handsome. *Good for Alan.* Lucas had practiced his carving skills.

Pouring bottled water into the man's face, he waited for Alan to come around.

"What? What the fuck?"

See, a criminal was just human and easy to get to. No one was above death, not even Alan.

"Hello, sunshine."

Alan didn't look a day older than thirty.

"Who the fuck are you?" Alan asked.

Smiling, Lucas grabbed a scalpel and impaled it in Alan's leg. The other man screamed, cursing.

"What the fuck?"

Removing the blade, he stabbed it into Alan's leg three more times. "So you are fucking human. People I've been talking to think you piss gold or some shit like that."

"You better release me before my men find me and fuck you up." Alan struggled against the restraints holding him.

"Good. The moment they get here, find you, I'll kill you." Lucas pulled out the two guns and placed them on the tray he'd set up with all of his instruments. "It's amazing really. You're not a very liked person. The people I spoke to were more than happy to give me everything I needed. You made a lot of enemies."

"Being king to the commoners means making enemies," Alan said, spitting onto the ground.

"You're king?"

"Someone needs to take care of the whores, the drugs, and the shit-heads."

"Yeah, I'm sure with your pretty face all the women come to you for help, and instead of getting heaven, you throw them into hell." Standing up, Lucas grabbed his knife from the back of his pocket. He walked behind Alan, grabbed him by the head, and slid the blade down Alan's face. "Let's see how many women want you near them when you look like a fucking monster."

For the next hour, Lucas worked over Alan's face. When he was done, he gripped the blade and slammed it into Alan's back, twisting the knife. The screams gave him little pleasure. It didn't matter how much Alan screamed. He wouldn't be getting Trevor back and Alan wasn't going to get his looks back.

Half way through the torture, Alan pissed himself. Not caring, Lucas pulled out the envelope Trevor left him.

Dear Lucas and Prue,

I fucked up big. I'm not going to make it through the night. I'm so sorry to you both for letting you down. I thought I was doing the right thing. I fucked up my delivery, and the others went back to Alan. They were working for him trying to get more money. Alan shot me, and now I'm fucking dying.

Lucas stopped reading as he saw the bloodstains. The writing was all over the place, the ink showing the pain Trevor had been in.

"Fuck, I can't feel my legs." Alan's voice was disjointed, showing his pain. His face was a fucking mess.

"Maybe I cut a nerve. Don't worry, it'll be years of physical therapy if you make it out of here alive," he said. Lucas shrugged, no longer giving a shit.

"What did I do to you?"

Ignoring the man, he went back to the letter.

Lucas, you were my brother. I have no choice but to beg you to take care of Prue. She needs you now more than ever. I've let you down as a friend, and now I've let you down as a brother. I'm so sorry. She needs to be looked after. I've kept her away from all this shit. If Alan ever finds out about her, it will be you and her he's after.

There's a rumor about him. When he goes after the people someone cares about he works out the number, and each time he marks one off, he reevaluates the number. There are three of us, so one down, two to go.

Please, be safe. I love you both, and I wish it could be different.

Love to you both,
Trevor

Folding up the letter, Lucas stared at Alan. The man was drooling from the mouth. "Trevor, he worked for you."

"I have a lot of Trevors working for me."

"Did you put a lot of bullets in men's guts in the last week?" Lucas asked.

"Ah, Trevor Lawson. He's got a sister and a best friend. I've been looking for them."

Slamming his fist into Alan's face, Lucas watched the other man crash to the floor. The chair held him in place. Ramming his foot into the man's stomach, Lucas lashed out, letting all the anger and rage out.

"You're meeting the friend now."

Lucas didn't stop until Alan was gasping for breath and trying to get him to stop. The man couldn't move. When he was done, he took the last of the petrol and doused Alan's body, the chair, and the fabric around him.

Lighting a match, he stared down at Alan.

"No one fucks with my family." Dropping the match, he didn't look back and left the building. He left the truck outside, climbed on his bike and headed back to Fort Wills to live his life.

Three weeks later he and Prue stood at an empty graveside with Trevor's name on it. She didn't live near

Fort Wills, and it had taken him time to get to her.

"I can't believe he's dead," she said.

To him she would always be Prue Lawson. To the outside world, she was Lilly Masters, a student preparing for a life of teaching youngsters.

"Neither can I," he said. He took hold of her hand, and together they would mourn for the loss of their friend. There was no one else to take care of them.

Prue was his responsibility, and he wasn't going to let her get hurt again.

ZERO

Chapter One

Present day

"Fuck, what are you doing? We need to get you to the hospital," Zero said, pressing his hands to the blood-soaked wound. Prue's eyes were wide as she looked at him, panicking. How the fuck was Alan back? He couldn't think about the other man. The only person he needed to care about was dying in his lap. No, he wouldn't accept it. Prue was not going to die. He'd already lost Trevor, and he wasn't going to lose Prue in the same way.

No more dying on his watch. He'd promised Trevor he'd care for her.

"What the fuck happened?" he asked, turning to Butch. The other man was covered in her blood.

"She was walking inside the compound. I was watching her. I recognized her but didn't know where from."

Tiny was barking out orders. Steven was on the phone. The sirens of an ambulance could be heard in the background. Sandy had stayed with Stink away from the clubhouse, and she wasn't on hand to help them. Fuck, why did they always need Sandy when she wasn't around?

"Come on, Prue. Don't fucking die on me."

"Someone fired a gun. No one else is hurt. None of us were close enough to the gate. Whoever was firing was aiming for her," Steven said, kneeling beside him.

"He … knows…" Prue gasped, and tears leaked out of the corners of her eyes.

"No, you're not going to die on me, do you hear? You don't get to fucking die on me." He couldn't think about Alan being back. The other man was supposed to be gone and dead.

"What the fuck is going on, Zero?" Tiny asked, glaring down at them.

He opened his mouth ready to spill everything, but the ambulance arrived. There was no time to tell him about the past. Later there would be more than enough time to bring Tiny and the others up to date. The only person who needed his attention right now was Prue. They loaded her onto a bed and carried her into the back.

"I'll tell you everything, but I need to be with her." He climbed in the back of the ambulance, not waiting for his brothers to say anything. Grabbing her hand, he watched the paramedic do what he needed to do.

Alan Lynch was alive. The only man who would leave a message like that was Alan. One night on the anniversary of Alan's death, Zero had gone to Prue, and in drink, he had told her everything about the past. She hated being kept in the dark, but she knew everything. He told her the truth from then on, never keeping anything from her. Prue was the first woman he was ever open and honest with, and not even Sophia made him feel that secure. Zero had told Prue what he did to Alan, the torture he'd inflicted on another person. She'd not judged him. Sophia was nothing like Prue.

Fuck, he'd almost kissed Sophia and gone over that line. Resting his head back against the truck, he kept hold of Prue's hand. The sudden commotion at the clubhouse had taken him away from Sophia. Part of him was pleased at the interruption. He didn't want to fuck up his place in the club.

They arrived at the hospital in ten minutes, breaking every speed limit. He followed them inside. A nurse pressed a hand to his chest, holding him back.

"Sir, you cannot go into the operating theater.

You've got to stay in the waiting room."

"She needs me."

"You're not a doctor or a surgeon. You will kill her if you don't do as I ask."

Nodding, he watched the blonde disappear through the clear doors, keeping him away. Heading back to the main reception, he signed in getting the necessary paperwork for Prue. He knew all of her details off by heart, both as Prue and as Lilly.

Staring down at his hands he saw they were covered in blood, Prue's blood. Memories of Trevor lying in his arms and his cutting off Trevor's air filled his mind. Shit, he was going to be sick.

Running to the bathroom, he spilled all the contents out of his stomach into the bottom of the toilet. Once he was done, he went to the sink, washing the blood, scrubbing his hands.

Butch walked in seconds later. Glancing at the door, Zero saw his friend was angry. His arms were folded over his chest. "You've got a lot of fucking explaining to do. I'm so fucking pissed right now."

"None of the club was killed. We're good." Zero scrubbed his hands, eyes going blurry at whose blood he was washing off. Torturing Alan, he'd gotten a lot of blood on his hands and hadn't cared.

Prue was not a criminal who deserved to die. She was a woman, a precious woman who should be left alone. He shouldn't be removing her blood from his hands. It was too much for him to take in.

"The boys are all outside. Tiny is outside waiting for an explanation. You're not going to get out of it, Zero. This shit is not how this works," Butch said. "The girl means something to you, doesn't she?"

"Yes, she does."

"Who is she? What is she to you, and why do I

recognize her?"

Scrubbing his hands clean, he stared at Butch, wiping his hands dry on towel. "She's my best friend's sister. I'm the one who is supposed to be taking care of her."

"None of this is making sense. You've never mentioned shit about her." Butch was not buying anything.

"I fucked up big."

"Why? How?" Butch asked.

"He'll not be telling you on your own," Tiny said, entering the bathroom. The other man was large, dominating, and brimming with rage. "We find out she is safe, and then we're having a meeting, and you're telling us everything."

"I can't leave her alone. She's in danger."

"Far as the person is concerned, she's dead," Tiny said.

"I can't risk it. I promised I'd keep her safe, and I've already fucked up."

"Then Blaine can stay behind. He's working on his shit with Emily and Darcy. It's time for him to do something for the club. Don't fucking question me again." Tiny left the bathroom, giving him no choice but to follow instruction.

Following behind the two men, Zero watched Tiny talk to Blaine, who nodded. His brothers were there, looking out for him. Running fingers through his hair he felt guilt swamp him as he looked at Nash. *Fuck.* He'd been about to kiss his wife.

Shit, fuck, shit. Killer was there as well. They were going to wait for the doctor to let them know how she was doing before leaving. He took a seat, staring at the clear doors, begging for the doctor to enter and give him some good news and to put him out of his misery.

He couldn't accept bad news right now.

Two down, one to go.

What the fuck was Alan even doing alive? Zero had left him for dead.

You didn't wait to see if he was dead.

Fuck.

Once he climbed on his bike, he hadn't waited to see if Alan died or not. He didn't care if he died himself or not, so long as Alan was no more. Once he'd set the match down, his thoughts had been directed toward Prue. For years afterward he kept returning to the city to see who was taking over from Alan. It was a surprise to see how many men came out of the woodwork to take over his place. None of the men were working for Alan or trying to take look for the man who got rid of Alan. Zero had fucked up, seeing as Alan was in fact alive.

Running a hand down his face, he looked toward the door. No one was coming, and he heard the chaos coming over the line as the hospital was taking in more emergency cases.

None of the brothers talked to him. Butch stayed sat beside him playing some game on his cell phone.

"I'm sorry," Zero said.

"I don't care. We'll handle whatever you've got to throw at us."

Closing his eyes, he rubbed at his temple, needing to know Prue was okay. This was going to take time. She needed to make a full recovery, as otherwise he failed Trevor.

Four hours later, the doctor appeared to give him the news.

"She's a lucky woman. The bullet didn't penetrate her heart or sever any major arteries. I extracted the bullet with ease. We'll keep an eye on her for the next couple of days in case of infection." The doctor nodded at all of them before leaving. Zero had already filled all the paperwork for her. Relief swamped him at the news. He wasn't going to lose her like he'd lost Trevor.

"Do you want to see her?" the nurse asked.

He nodded, following her down to the ICU. "Why is she here?"

"To keep her under observation. We'll keep an eye on her all through the night and move her to a ward tomorrow morning."

Zero moved to her bedside. There was a tube inside her mouth, and she was hooked up to other tubes and drips. He didn't know what all the machines did, but they must be helping her in some way. She was breathing on her own, which he was thankful for.

The nurse left him alone as he stared down into Prue's pale face. Reaching out he stroked her red hair away from her face. She was such a beautiful woman. He'd always found her striking, and he struggled to look away from her whenever he was in her company. Why was he suddenly thinking about her beauty? It was wrong with her lying in a hospital bed. "Hey, honey. You've got to fight this and live. Live for me. I promise, I will not fail you again. You're not going anywhere. I'll take care of you and love you."

He leaned down, kissing her temple.

She didn't respond. Her face pale making her red hair stand out even more, Prue was a beautiful woman, and he was surprised she wasn't taken. Any man with any sense would snatch her right up. *He* would, given half a chance.

"I'm sorry," he said, brushing his lips against her temple once again.

Prue stayed silent, sleeping.

She's only sleeping.

He needed to remember she was only sleeping and there was nothing else wrong with her.

Staring around the hospital room, Zero didn't know what he was going to do. After a few minutes he left her side going back toward the main reception of the hospital. He was tired of being near the hospital. In the last few years he felt he'd lived more at the hospital than the clubhouse. The Skulls had dealt with their fair share of enemies, each one hurting a member at one point. They had even lost some of their own men because of those enemies. What was Alan going to do to him or The Skulls? Cutting the thoughts off, he made his way out of the hospital. He hadn't brought his bike and ended up climbing on the back of Butch's bike. Blaine was staying at the hospital to take care of Prue while Zero was due back at the clubhouse for the meeting. Butch waited outside, standing beside his bike. Nash and a few others had stayed behind.

"Don't get any fucking ideas. My ass is my own," Butch said, pointing at his bike.

Rolling his eyes, Zero held onto his friend while his thoughts were with Prue. She was a teacher and took care of young children, first grade he believed. Shit, what the fuck was he going to do? Prue shouldn't be dead or even fighting for her life.

They arrived at the clubhouse. On the way inside he saw Sophia waiting up with her daughter. Her gaze landed on him then turned to Nash. He saw her cheeks were heated, but her smile held all the warmth for her husband, not for him. Once Nash was inside, Sophia didn't look back toward him. She didn't give him any clue as to what she thought.

She's not looking at you because she doesn't want you. This is her answer.

Hating the kick to the gut he experienced he

entered Tiny's office, sitting at the table in the middle of the room. The other members made their way into the room.

His thoughts returned to Trevor's death ten years ago. No matter how hard he tried, Zero never got away from the memories. They haunted him wherever he went. No man should have to take his friend's life. If Alan lived, why did he wait ten years to take him out?

Two down, one to go.

Zero wasn't afraid of death and hadn't been for a long time. Providing he took Alan out with him, Zero would welcome death with open fucking arms.

The door slammed closed. He didn't respond staring at the center of the table.

"Start fucking talking," Tiny said.

Zero blinked as his thoughts collided into one. "Ten years ago I got a call from my best friend. He wasn't part of The Skulls, but he was my family. He'd been working for a man known as Alan Lynch." Zero stopped as the pain returned once again. Trevor should have lived. Burying his best friend should never have happened, and neither should have holding him in those last moments with no way to help him.

For the next thirty minutes he told all of The Skulls what he had done. He didn't leave a single detail out from the torture and finally walking away after setting Alan on fire.

"He was supposed to be dead," Zero said.

"Then what makes you think he's alive?"

Pulling out the card Prue gave to him, he placed it in the center of the table. He listened as they all read it. "Trevor told me it was his signal. Alan goes after all the family. Prue and myself are all that remains for Trevor. He was young and didn't have the time to create a family. It has been ten years, but Alan's picking up where he left off, and he won't stop until Prue and I stop breathing."

Gritting his teeth, Zero forced the tears back. He wouldn't cry in front of his brothers. They needed him to be strong. The tears were not for fear of his death; they were for what he'd lost and the woman lying in the hospital.

"Why wait ten years?" Steven asked, hands folded over his chest.

"That's what I want to know," Tiny said.

"I fucked him up big. He wouldn't have gotten out of there easily. There has to have been something I overlooked."

"Someone looking like a monster will be noticed, Zero," Tiny said.

"Not necessarily," Whizz said. "It's easy in this day and age to get lost. Look what happened with Snitch, and that fucker wasn't even trying. Alan had the money to change his face and start over. No one is looking for Alan Lynch as he's presumed dead. Why go looking for a dead man?"

"Fuck." Tiny cursed, stepping away to look outside the window. "We don't have a clue why this fucker waited so long. Why didn't you come to us?" he asked, turning back to glare at him. "You were a prospect and could have come to us at any time. Why didn't you?"

"I was new, and I didn't want to get you involved in my shit. I had no intention of coming back," Zero said.

"What?" Butch asked.

"I didn't know if I was going to survive, and to be honest, I didn't care."

The others around him cursed.

"I was a prospect. I wasn't going to bring you in on my mess. My best friend had died in my arms. The only thing I wanted to do was take out the fucker who did it and threatened Prue. I did what I set out to do. I protected her, or at least I thought I protected her, but I didn't because he's back."

"You were twenty-three years old," Tiny said. "A fucking baby."

"I've been firing a gun since I was ten and fighting at fifteen. I took him out, and I didn't care if I lived or died. He killed my best friend. Trevor died in my arms, and he asked one thing from me, to keep his sister safe, and I failed." Zero repeated himself so the club would understand that he did what he'd had to do. If he could go back he wouldn't change a fucking thing, apart from watching the building burn to the ground.

He stood up, fisting his hands begging for something to hurt. As he paced the room, the anger was filling him. Whenever this happened he went out on his bike.

"I need to get out of here."

"You're not going anywhere," Tiny said.

Zero felt the crew's eyes on him. Slamming his fist against the wall, he lashed out needing to feel the bite of pain from the hit.

"Take him down to the gym," Tiny said. "You want to fight then the brothers will fight you back."

****

Prue hurt all over. It hurt to move, and she was so scared as she opened her eyes. She thought about her brother and then frowned. Trevor was dead. He wasn't going to be coming to help her. What the hell had happened? Opening her eyes, she looked around the dark hospital room, scared, terrified, and shocked.

Where was she? Her memories were all fuzzy.

"Hello, Prue." The voice that spoke was dark, filled with danger. She didn't recognize the voice, but she heard the threat inside it. No one besides Zero knew her real name. Waking up, she started to become aware of herself, the blankness disappearing as all of her memories returned in full force. Zero was the main focus of her thoughts. Prue remembered she'd been on the way to see him. She knew he only went by Zero now, not Lucas. The night her brother died, so had Lucas. "You must mean so much to Zero. He posted a guard inside the hospital, but it's so easy getting around when you wear the right uniform. This hospital sure needs a lot of money and resources. The place is understaffed on every front."

She looked around the darkened room trying to find the owner of the voice. "Who are you? What do you want?" she asked. The machine monitoring her heart showed her fear. Her heart was racing. The pain increased, and she saw a clip had been placed on the morphine that was supposed to be going into her body to ease the pain.

"I'm not anything of importance," he said, getting to his feet. "In fact, we've never actually met. I never got that privilege years ago." She saw the outline of him as he came into view, and she gasped.

His face was distorted. The faded silver lines showed so many scars, but there were also scars that he couldn't get rid of, burn marks down one side of his face. "Ah, I see you know who I am now. I'm surprised Zero told you about what happened. He was so determined to protect you. Your little boyfriend thought no one would come to my aid. I'm going to show him what real pain feels like." He reached out to touch her face.

Tears filled her eyes. "Alan?"

"The very one, but I'm not as pretty as I used to be. Another thing to add to the list of things to thank Zero for. He's not going by Lucas anymore, I must remember that. He's Zero now. Strange name if you ask me."

"You're dead," she said, whimpering. His finger was running up and down her cheek. She couldn't move. The fear tightened inside her, gripping her. She was held in place by that very fear. Zero told her all about what he'd done to this man. Prue thought he was dead, yet here he was, ready to hurt her.

"I was dead, or at least he thought I was dead," Alan said, looking down at her, smiling. She'd never seen a look so evil before in her life. "Zero needs to learn to check or watch when he's killed someone. I wasn't dead, and there was someone special in my life who dragged me out of the building. She saved me."

Who would save this monster?

"You killed my brother."

"He was selling me out. I treated him like I do all traitors. I kill them. It wasn't personal. Trevor knew what he was getting into, and if he didn't, then he was a fucking fool. A dead fool now."

She whimpered as his fingers glided around her neck. He could kill her so easily.

"I can feel your pulse." His fingers caressed over the pulse in her neck, the threat there in every touch. "It would be so easy to take all that away. No one is here to stop me or to protect you. You're at my mercy to do with as I please."

Reaching up, she gripped his arm, trying to stop him. "Please, don't."

"I've been watching you, Prue. You're innocent. It's a shame really. If it wasn't for your brother and Zero, I would have left you alone." He tightened his grip cutting off her air supply. Scratching at his arm, she panicked, the pain making it hard for her to struggle. Alan leaned in close. "I was going to give him a quick death, but after everything I've gone through, the years of pain and getting back to where I am, I'm going to take my time."

His lips were so close to her ear.

Her vision was getting blurry, but he suddenly released his hold. His hand lay around her neck, but there was nowhere else for her to go. Whatever he had planned, she would have to take it, hoping that Zero would save her again.

"I'm going to play a game, and you're going to be a messenger," he said. His hand glided down her neck to land on her breast. She cried out, going to stop him from touching her. A knife landed against her throat. "I don't think so, pet. You will let me do what I want, or I will make it hurt a hell of a lot better."

"Please," she said, hating herself for begging her brother's killer for mercy. "Don't kill me."

"You're in no position to beg, baby. Now, release my hand."

Hands shaking, she moved away, fisting her palms at her sides. She sank her nails into her skin, trying to find some sanity over what was happening.

This was why Zero tried to kill him and failed. Tears spilling out of her eyes, she bit into her lip to stop herself from calling out.

"I'm surprised Zero hasn't fucked you. You're so fucking beautiful," he said.

She was disgusted with him. His hand moved down her body drawing the blanket down with him.

Nails sinking into her flesh, she closed her eyes trying to find a happy place as his hand covered her mound.

Don't think. Don't think. Don't think.

Feeling ill she concentrated on the blade of his knife against her neck.

He touched her over the hospital gown. "See, all you need is the right incentive to give me what I want," he said. "I could fuck you right here and now, and all it would take is the blade against your throat to let me."

Not making a noise, she prayed for a nurse to find her and to take him away.

Please, please, please.

She chanted the words over and over again, begging for some relief. Prue was happy for anyone to come to her rescue and stop him.

"However, I will fuck you when the time is right." He removed the blade and replaced the blanket over her legs.

Opening her eyes, she saw he was smiling. The tears fell thick and fast from her eyes. "Why won't you just kill me and get it over with?" Her voice broke, and she felt like such a coward.

"Why do that when I can have so much fun keeping you alive?" Alan gazed across the room. She saw he was thinking. What did Zero do to him to make him so vicious? Wait, she knew what he did, but why was he back now? *Fuck.* Her thoughts were all over the place. Had Zero told her the truth, or had he kept some of the shit he'd done to Alan from her? "You know, Zero taught me something ten years ago. He taught me that patience can make this game fun."

"Game?"

"Consider it a game of cat and mouse. Guess what you are?" he asked.

The evil lurking in his eyes kept her quiet.

"The game is going to begin. I hope Zero is ready for what I'm about to do." Alan leaned down, invading her space once again. "You're going to be so much fun. I see now who I can use to make him suffer."

"Why wait all these years?" she asked.

"There's nothing like waiting to make the game so much sweeter. Enjoy what you've got left of your life,

Prue. It's going to be fucking fun." He kissed her head and left.

When he left she panicked and started to scream. The nurse charged in, releasing the clip on her morphine. A man covered in ink and wearing The Skulls leather jacket entered the room.

"What's going on?" he asked, staring from her to the nurse.

"You shouldn't be in here," the nurse said.

"I don't give a fuck."

Prue was panicking. She was scared of what was about to happen. Whatever Alan had planned, he was going to relish every second of making them both suffer.

"Get Zero. Please, I need him. Get Zero."

The biker nodded and left the room.

"You need to calm down, honey."

"No, I need him. Please, he needs to know what's going on."

Another doctor entered the room. Her heart was racing. Perspiration dotted her brow.

I have to get out of here. Zero is in danger. I've got to warn him.

"What's going on?" the doctor asked.

"She's panicking. We need to calm her down."

Prue shook her head. She couldn't speak as she struggled to breathe. No, she couldn't calm down. Alan could get to her no matter where she was. No one cared. The only person she could trust was Zero. Where was he? Why wasn't he here? A mask was placed over her mouth, and she was eased down on the bed. Staring at the nurse she saw the nurse was telling her to calm down, but Prue couldn't hear the words.

She couldn't be calm. The sudden sting in her arm had her gasping. Slowly, ever so slowly she started to feel heavy.

No, I have to warn Zero. He is in danger. We are both in danger.
****

Butch sat at the bar sipping a whiskey as he thought about all he'd heard. He remembered the time Zero was talking about as he'd been shouting at him over the phone. He always wondered what happened to his friend during that time, but once Zero returned, he never asked. Thinking back, he recalled the change within him, which had to be down to losing his best friend. Closing his eyes, he took a swallow of the liquid as he felt arms band around him. "Hey, baby, are you ready for a fuck?"

Opening his eyes, he glanced behind him at the sweet-butt hanging off him. She had long, dyed blonde hair and was wearing a short skirt and bikini top. All of her body was on display leaving nothing to the imagination. He'd played with Carla many times. She liked to fuck hard, but he wasn't in the mood for fucking or doing anything. Zero was in trouble. Butch needed to keep his shit about him for whatever was about to go down.

"No, go and fuck another brother," he said, shrugging her off.

"I don't want to. My pussy wants you."

Shaking his head, he moved away from the bar and left the clubhouse. He needed a ride. Getting onto his bike, he left the compound. Butch wasn't wearing a helmet, and he made his way into town without any trouble. Straddling his bike he watched the people who were going about their business, walking, talking, romancing and shit.

Fuck, none of them were having to deal with a new enemy. Most of the people in Fort Wills were worrying about the mundane shit. Zero would never be on his own again. His enemy was the club's enemy.

Getting off his bike, Butch walked through town, going around the back of the shops, and he stopped short when he saw the church in his sights. He'd never been to church. Neither had any of the brothers, apart from when they had gone for Angel's wedding.

He entered the church grounds and saw the door was open, spilling light out into the night. There lay plenty of gravestones on his way toward the door, leaving him depressed. So much death surrounded him and The Skulls at present. How were they all supposed to survive?

What the fuck are you doing?

Ignoring the voice inside his head, he entered the church. No one was inside, but the altar was alight with several candles. Sitting at the back, he stared at the statue in front of him. Something about Zero's story made Butch feel sick. Whoever was after Zero wasn't going to play by the rules. Butch didn't know how he knew this, only that he did. Someone who waited ten years wasn't going to play nice, and this was going to be different for all of them, not just Zero.

Ten years of hatred, the scars, the pain. Alan, whoever he was, would make Zero pay ten times over. The club was going to be hurting by the time this was all over.

A feminine hum filled the air. Glancing to the side he watched a woman with long brown hair enter the church. She wasn't wearing religious clothing but a pair of jeans and a plain white shirt. It was late, but she was carrying an armful of books. Her hair was pulled back into a simple ponytail. The length fell below her ass, her hair was so long.

She was curvy as well. The shirt highlighted her full tits and small waist as it clung to her skin.

When she turned around, he heard her gasp.

"I'm so sorry. I'll be quiet and leave you to your prayers," she said, turning away.

"No, you don't need to leave. I wasn't praying." He stood up then sat down as he didn't want to scare her.

"Why come to church if you don't want to pray? Would you like me to get the Father?" she asked, pointing to the door.

"Are you a nun?" he asked.

"No, I work in town at the florists' shop, and for fun I help out here," she said. He watched as she took several steps toward him. She held the books against her chest like a lifeline.

"You shouldn't tell anyone about yourself. Some people would take advantage."

Her cheeks went bright red, and she withdrew her hand.

"Sorry. My mom says I need to learn to shut up a bit." She smiled even though it didn't reach her eyes.

"Shit, I'm sorry. Crap, now I'm cursing in church."

She giggled. "Don't worry about it. I'm sure He'll forgive you."

Smiling, Butch was curious about her. "What's your name?"

"I'm Cheryl Barnes. It's nice to meet you."

"Butch, I'm a member of The Skulls," he said, taking her hand. Her hand was so soft and tiny inside his. What the fuck was happening to him?

"I know of The Skulls. It's nice to meet you, Butch." She handed him a Bible and turned to leave.

"Where did you say you worked?"

"At the florist. I've made several arrangements for Lash and Tiny. They like my arrangements. It's nice to meet you." She made her way back to leave Bibles in her wake.

ZERO

Well, fuck him.

Chapter Two

"What the hell happened?" Zero asked, entering the hospital. Blaine was standing inside the reception area. The moment he got the call he stopped fighting with his brothers to get down to the hospital. Prue was far more important than his need to get his ass kicked.

"I don't know. She had a massive panic attack and started calling for you. The doctors have sedated her," Blaine said. "Nothing would calm her down."

"Prue doesn't have panic attacks. She's always dealt with everything straight away," he said. Going toward the ICU he brushed past the nurses and went to her bedside. She was sleeping, and he couldn't see anything wrong with her. It was like nothing had changed from the moment he last saw her.

Taking one of her hands inside his, he looked down to see the bruising of her nails. She'd dug them into her fist hard enough to leave bruises. What the fuck? Prue wasn't like this. None of this made sense to him, not the panic attacks or the bruises on her hands. Something had to have happened to scare her.

"What happened to you?" he asked, trying to figure everything out.

"She's not going to wake up for some time," the doctor said. "We had to sedate her, but she will be okay."

"I'm not leaving."

"I insist you leave."

"No, the last time I left she had a panic attack. I'm not leaving her side, and you're not going to make me." He glared at the doctor ready to commit murder if they didn't listen to him. A couple of hours he was gone and something had happened. There was no way he was leaving her now. Prue needed him.

The doctor stared at him for several minutes and

then left. Grabbing the chair in the far corner Zero dragged it toward the bed.

"Hey, Prue. I'm here. Nothing is going to happen to you." He kept talking to her, holding her hand tightly.

He'd failed her again. Something wasn't right. Prue never panicked. Even when her parents died, she hadn't panicked.

"The Skulls know everything. They're going to help us, baby." Cutting off his speech, he tried to fight back the sudden need to cry.

Fuck, he wasn't a pussy, and he refused to cry. Prue and his club needed him strong. Breaking down and crying wasn't going to solve any of the problems he now had.

Sitting back in his chair he thought about Trevor. Since they were little they had taken care of Prue. Where his parents didn't give a fuck about him, Prue and Trevor's parents had been the opposite. The fatal shooting that had taken their lives had hit the brother and sister hard. Zero had been there to help them both heal. At the time Prue had been a mere fifteen years old. A teenager, dealing with all kinds of shit, then her parents' death on top of that, and she'd survived it all. Trevor didn't want to send her to care, but he also didn't have the first clue how to look after or protect her.

Rubbing at his temples, Zero remembered so many fond memories with all of them. Three weeks after their parents' funeral Trevor had been drunk out of his face and Prue was having nightmares. Zero's parents didn't give a fuck about him, and being over eighteen he didn't need to stay with them. Most of his time was spent at Trevor's, where he could take care of the two people who meant the world to him.

When his sporadic visits no longer helped, Zero started staying at their house all the time to give them much needed support when he could. Prue had been so scared, screaming in her sleep. Zero recalled walking into her bedroom, wrapping his arms around her. She jerked awake fighting him. Throughout the fight he held onto her, calming her down.

"I hate them, Lucas. I hate them for leaving me." She cried, holding onto him as she sobbed her heart out.

"I know, honey. I know. We're going to be here for you."

"I'm scared."

"There's no need to be scared. I'm here, and while I'm here Trevor will never do anything stupid. Your brother loves you."

At the time he'd kissed her head and stayed with her, falling asleep with his arms wrapped around her. In the morning, he'd been gone before she could wake up. For several months after the funeral he ended up spending a lot of time in her bed until the nightmares stopped.

Zero also recalled missing the feel of her as she slept when it stopped. He'd cut that yearning shit out. Fifteen year old Prue was not ever going to be in his fantasies. But staring at her now, he couldn't deny the beauty she'd turned into.

She was always so smart, beautiful, and had a fun wit about her. Growing up Prue had been a bit of a tomboy, preferring to get dirty with them than dressing it up with makeup.

"Come on, Prue. Fight this," he said.

Around four he left her side to grab himself a coffee. He stood at the vending machine, rubbing his eyes. Zero was so tired, but he forced himself to stay awake. Blaine had gone home. He didn't see the point to the both of them being without sleep. The only person capable of calming Prue down was him.

"Hey," a feminine voice said.

Glancing to the side he saw a beautiful, short haired blonde dressed in a nurse's outfit.

"Hey," he said, lifting the Styrofoam to his lips. Zero knew what she was after. Her gaze kept going to his leather cut then traveling down his body to land at his crotch. "Honey, what do you want?"

She pressed a hand to his chest, glancing around. The reception area was empty, which was strange. A hospital should have plenty of staff, right? The lights were dimmed, and the dark night showed outside. The hospital felt eerie to him considering it was supposed to be a comfortable place to make people better.

"I was wondering how I could attract a Skull? I've been curious about you for years."

Zero hadn't fucked a woman in a long time. The last woman he was with was on the night he, Steven, and Killer were having a drink. Since then his sex life had consisted of him thinking about Sophia while beating off with his fist. Fuck, he was feeling horny. The nurse's tits were large and her body tight. Putting his full coffee into the trash, he grabbed her hand and led the nurse to the nearest bathroom. He stormed into the female bathroom, which was empty. Going into the nearest stall, he yanked the nurse inside.

"Please," she said, moaning.

Her hand landed on his cock. He was rock hard, but it wasn't for her.

Pushing her to the wall, he shoved her pants down to her ankles. Gripping a condom from his pocket, he unzipped his jeans, sheathed himself and pulled her hips toward him. He always carried a condom. No brat was going to be born because of his lack of protection. Finding her molten heat, he slid a finger deep inside her core, feeling her grip him tightly.

"Fuck, you want it, don't you, baby?"

"Yes, fuck me, please."

This was not unusual for him. A lot of women approached them at one time or another begging for a fuck. He preferred women dripping wet to fuck. There was nothing good about a dry pussy and a woman not interested. This woman had sweet-butt material written all over her. Replacing his fingers with his cock, he aligned the tip and slammed deep inside her.

She cried out, resting her palms against the wall of the stall. He pummeled in and out of her, stroking her clit as he worked his dick inside her. There was no passion inside him, only a need to get off. Zero closed his eyes thinking about Sophia, but her image was instantly replaced by Prue's. Her red hair, fanned out around her, along with her kind green eyes, smiling back.

Fuck. Cutting the thought off, he opened his eyes and stared at the back of the woman he was fucking. The need to orgasm was what drove him higher to the peak. Biting his lip, he fucked her hard, using her cunt for his own pleasure.

When she found her release, he didn't care. This had nothing to do with anyone else but him.

Slamming in deep he released his cum into the condom before stepping away. With women like this, Zero didn't linger too long. He hated for bitches to get the wrong idea about what he wanted. Peeling the latex off his cock, he wrapped it in tissue and threw it down the toilet. Zero made sure to flush the condom away. He'd heard of women trying to stake a claim on other men by using filled condoms. Again, he wasn't having any brats he didn't want. Taking some more tissue he cleaned off his cock before tucking himself away. She was pulling up her pants as he zipped up his jeans. Zero had lost interest in the woman. All he wanted to do was get back to Prue's side.

"Thank you for that," she said, breathless. Her cheeks were red, but he wasn't ready to wait around. "I've always been curious about club cock. Will you put in a good word for me at the club?"

"No, the men will fuck you if you want it. It's up to you to do the rest."

He left the bathroom, grabbing another coffee and making his way back to Prue's bedside. She was still asleep. The doctor had sedated her so she wouldn't be waking up anytime soon. Sitting in the chair beside her bed, he watched her sleep, thinking about the nurse. He shouldn't have fucked her, not with Prue hurting in the hospital. Fuck, he felt guilty now.

Sipping his coffee, he stared at her and waited for sanity to return. Why had she replaced Sophia's face? For so long he'd been wanting Nash's woman, and now she was replaced. No, he didn't have a thing for Prue. She was sweet, loving, and his deceased friend's sister. He wasn't going to do anything with Prue.

Sophia. Sitting back, he closed his eyes thinking about her dark hair and blue eyes. She was so perfect … so taken. Nash didn't deserve for him to take his woman. *Could you really take Sophia away from him?*

Again, Prue invaded his thoughts, annoying him. Cutting the thoughts aside, he finished off his coffee, throwing the empty cup away. The coffee was rancid, and he needed the good stuff. When he couldn't get comfortable on the chair, he saw there was plenty of room on one side of Prue.

It had been a long time since he'd held her. He really needed to hold her now to make sure she was really alive. What was wrong with him sleeping beside her? Zero had held her all through the night when her parents died. This was no different.

Only, you're having sexy thoughts about her whereas when she was fifteen you didn't.

Hesitating, he watched Prue sleeping. Was it wrong for him to hold her?

He got to his feet and sat beside her, making sure all the wires hooked up to her were out of the way. Sliding an arm underneath her head, he brought her toward his chest, getting her to lie against him.

"It's okay, baby, I've got you," he said. Her heat surrounded him.

Wrapping his arms around her, he settled down on the bed, stroking her hair. The smell of the hospital was replaced by the scent of Prue. The feel of her against him comforted in ways he'd not felt in a long time.

"I'm so sorry for putting you in danger, Prue."

She didn't respond, and he felt like a complete bastard. How did Alan know where to look for her? How did Alan survive what he did?

Fuck. He'd turned his back on the man dying without checking to see if he was alive or dead. Lighting the match and setting fire to Alan, he'd not waited around to see if anyone went inside the building or came out. It was his mistake.

His body started to feel sluggish as the lack of sleep finally caught up with him. Rubbing a hand down his face, he looked up at the ceiling, thinking of ways to stay awake.

Don't fall asleep. Stay awake.

Zero glanced down staring at her shocking red hair. She really was a beauty. Was there a man waiting for her back at home? When he visited her after The Darkness attacked him she hadn't been with anyone. Much could change in over a year. He hated the thought of another man being in her life, meaning something to her.

Surely Prue wasn't dating anyone.

Why wouldn't she be dating anyone? She's a fucking beauty.

Jealousy spiked through him at the thought of any other man touching her. Prue was never supposed to be with anyone.

Closing his eyes, Zero could not hold sleep off any longer and drifted off to sleep with Prue in his arms. His guard was down to anything but the feel of her back with him. Peace.

****

Heat surrounded Prue making her feel comforted for the first time since she'd lost her parents. Opening her eyes, she felt sluggish, and the pain was no longer there. She looked across to see Zero passed out beside her on the hospital bed. Everything that happened last night came crashing through her. Jerking up, she gasped as the sudden jolt sent a hard pain through her chest where she'd been shot. Fuck, she'd been shot, and Alan had been here.

"Prue, honey, what's the matter?" Zero asked, waking up.

Tears filled her eyes as she stared back at him. "Alan's back."

He sat up, climbing off the bed. "What do you mean? I know he's the one who shot you, but do you mean he's back?"

She nodded, wiping the tears from her cheeks. Her glasses were gone, and she was struggling to see without them. "Yes, he was here last night." She'd never have dreamt something so disturbing. Alan was in her room, threatening Zero by using her.

"In your room?"

"Yes, he was here last night, Zero." She recalled his touch with disgust. "He's a monster."

"I know."

"No, you don't. He said he's waited ten years, and now he's going to enjoy playing this game. Why wait ten years, and why is he playing games? Why doesn't he just kill us?" The words filled her with dread even though she had to say them.

"He was inside your room last night?"

"Yes."

"Fuck. Blaine didn't even have a clue anyone was in your room until you were screaming."

"Why wait all this time?" Prue asked.

"I don't know. He said something about playing a game?"

"Yeah. The game of cat and mouse where we're the mouse."

"I've not got a clue, Prue. I don't know why he waited, and I don't know what he's got planned."

"He's scarred, Zero, and scary." She swallowed at what he'd done. There had been nothing she could do to stop Alan's touch.

Looking up at Zero, she saw the anger in his face. "What did he do and say?"

She told him everything that happened from the touching to the words. She didn't leave anything out even as Zero cursed, slamming his fist into the wall. Looking at him, she saw his knuckles were bloody and bruised. There were no bruises on his face though, and he gave no sign that he was in pain.

"Why are your hands cut up?" she asked, feeling nervous.

"I got into a fight last night." He lifted up his shirt to show her some of the bruises. They were hard to make out as his stomach and chest were covered in ink. He was like a walking talking advertisement for tattoo parlors. Where there was tanned skin, she saw the purple bruising. "He's going to play a game?"

Swallowing past the lump in her throat, Prue nodded. "He's going to kill us, but he's going to make it last so you're hurting, Zero. This is going to be nothing more than a game to him."

Lifting her hand to her neck, she stroked the pulse at the side. Alan had cut off her air supply so easily. He could have killed her last night. She knew whatever he had planned was going to hurt a lot more than last night ever had.

"I'm not leaving you alone," he said.

"Good. You posted a guard outside, and it didn't stop Alan from getting inside."

"He's scarred?"

"Yes, you really messed up his face. When you told me what you did, I didn't think it was that bad. You really went to town on him, didn't you?"

"He killed Trevor. I wasn't going to let him get away with it."

She wiped the tears from her eyes. There was nothing either of them could do. Alan was going to play his game. "Could you do me a favor and phone the school to let them know it's going to be a few weeks before I return? I'm not going to risk him hurting the children, and it's not like I can go back."

"He's capable of anything."

She watched him pull out his cell phone. "Who are you calling?"

"Tiny and the club. They need to know he was here."

"Why?" she asked.

"He got past Blaine without anyone knowing and the security at the hospital. Not only did he do that, but he was able to hurt you when no one was around. I don't accept shit like that."

She was touched by his caring. The nurse bustled into the room, glanced at Zero and clucked her tongue. "You don't use that here."

Zero glared.

"Go make your call." Prue was petrified at being alone. Alan had been in her life twenty-four hours, and she was already scared to be alone. How pitiful was that?

"Are you sure?"

"Yeah, I need to learn to be alone again."

He moved to her bedside, leaning down to kiss her temple. "I'll be back before you know it."

She watched him leave the room as the nurse started working around her, reading her charts and taking her blood pressure. Prue stayed silent, closing her eyes as the fright began to grip her.

He's not here. He's not coming for me.

Prue knew it would only be a matter of time before he came for her. Whatever Alan was planning it wasn't going to be nice.

"You'll be moving to a ward later today," the nurse said.

"Okay."

"Your man, he shouldn't be here. We've got visiting hours for a reason."

The woman walked away, leaving the clipboard on the end of her bed.

Didn't stop a maniac from coming to my room, fucking bitch.

This was the first time she'd been in the hospital for any length of time.

"Tiny and the boys will be here soon. You're moving to a ward?"

"Yeah, the nurse was a bit of a bitch."

"Don't trust the nurses." He took a seat on her bed, smiling down at her.

"I bet you've fucked all the nurses here."

"Not all of them." He frowned. "Is there a man at your place I need to get in touch with? I'd hate for someone to be worried."

"No, there's no man." She had been with two men in her whole life. The first guy hadn't lasted a week after taking her virginity before Trevor got a hold of him. After him, there was a guy who worked at a bar, but apart from the lust there was nothing else between them. She loved sex, yet she wanted something more, something deeper. Sex as an act could be quite boring without the passion. Maybe she was fucked in the head. A lot of people could fuck without needing something more.

"I'm surprised. I thought there'd be loads of men knocking at your door."

"I've not been in a relationship in a long time. Trevor saw to that when we were younger. Any guy knocking on the door and he sent them away. Getting older, I've not had the time or desire to be with anyone." She stopped, biting her lip. Thinking about Trevor always left her filled with pain. Never a moment went by when she didn't think about him. Being around Zero reminded her of what she'd lost. The only other guy she'd been with since Trevor's death was the guy at the bar, and she'd only gone to him to scratch an itch.

"I miss him, too," he said. "I tried to get him to join The Skulls with me. He said he had other plans."

"We both know what other plans he had." She gasped at the pain his absence brought. "I can't talk about him. It hurts too much."

Zero took her hand, brushing some hair off her face. "We'll get through this. He would kill me for what I let happen to you."

"What did happen to me?" she asked, staring

down her body then at the machines.

"Someone drove by and shot you. No one else was killed or hurt." Zero hung his head. "I was so fucking stupid. I shouldn't have come to you when I did."

She knew he was referring to the time he had to hide out from another MC group, The Darkness, she recalled. His visit had been the highlight of her year even though he'd spent most of the time worried about his club.

"No, you don't get to blame yourself for what happened. You needed me, and we both promised each other to be there for each other."

"I could have gone anywhere else."

"Stop," she said. "Stop making this all about you. You didn't get shot, and you were not the one lying here waiting for him to finish whatever he wanted to do." She looked away unable to meet the pity in his gaze.

"You won't be alone again."

A woman cleared her throat. Prue glanced toward the door to see a blonde eating Zero up. Looking at Zero she knew instantly that he'd fucked her. The interest in the nurse's eyes wasn't hard to see.

A sharp pang cut through her chest. Zero would fuck everything that walked. She had learned from a young age never to expect anything from him, which was why she'd never waited for him.

"It's time to move you," the nurse said.

Getting up from the bed, Zero moved to the far wall not looking at her. Another nurse entered, and then she was being wheeled out of the unit. She was used to being around women who fucked Zero. None of them ever stayed around, and she'd never known for him to settle down with a woman and rarely saw him with the same one twice. Zero walked behind her. The woman who entered first was still eating him up. Her whole body showed how much she wanted him whereas Zero wasn't giving her the time of day. In fact, it looked like he didn't remember her.

Locking her fingers together, Prue stared up at the ceiling that passed. The only time she'd ever really been close to Zero was when her parents died. She'd been suffering from the worst nightmares of her life. They terrified her, giving her night terrors, leaving her afraid to sleep. Zero would hold her tight, sleep beside her, and the night terrors soon disappeared.

She hated being an inconvenience. The moment she stopped needing him, he walked away. He never stayed at the house after that apart from when he was too intoxicated to leave.

He stood beside the wall as they entered the private room.

"I can't afford the private room. I thought I was going to a ward." Her insurance only handled so much of her care while she paid for the rest.

"The Skulls is paying for this care," he said.

The nurses got her settled and left. The blonde lingered a little too long for Prue's taste.

"Leave," Zero said.

Prue watched her walk out shooting a glare toward her. She stared at the woman, wondering what she expected. Bedding a biker doesn't guarantee you'll be in his life forever. Nothing guaranteed staying in Zero's life.

"You fucked her." She turned back to look at him.

He nodded. His cheeks were red tinted.

"Are you embarrassed?" she asked, smiling. She needed to smile rather than cry. None of her emotions made any sense. Zero was a friend, nothing more.

Do you want him to be something extra?

"No, I'm not. I fuck who I want."

Nodding, she sat up on the bed. Her stomach growled, and it was her turn to feel her cheeks heating.

"Breakfast will be along shortly."

"Thank you," she said, glancing at him.

"For what?"

"For being here for me. You're the only person I know I can trust."

He looked at the floor. "Prue, you can always come to me. I don't care when, where, or how, I will always be here for you."

His cell phone went off, interrupting their conversation. "I'll be back soon."

She watched him leave, missing him the moment he left the room.

Chapter Three

Zero found Tiny, Butch, Steven, and a couple of the others waiting outside in the waiting room. He shook Tiny's hand and led him back toward Prue's room. He was so nervous about Alan and told him everything that happened last night. They entered the room, and Prue had a plate in front of her. He stopped as she took a bite of banana. Her lips molded around the tip, and he was struck by the sudden image of his cock in her mouth. Heat filled his cock, and all he wanted to do was push the others out of the room and take her.

Shoving the images aside, he took a step inside.

"Hey," she said, wiping her lips, putting the banana skin down on the tray. Her breakfast was nowhere near finished.

"This is Tiny, Prue." Zero made the introductions. She nodded at each of them. He hated the way her gaze lingered on Steven. The other man was not up for sex, at least not when it came to Prue. She was off the market. Zero wouldn't allow Steven anywhere near her. The desire to find the other two men who'd touched her and fuck them up was strong. Gritting his teeth, he saw Steven linger as he shook her hand.

"It's a pleasure to meet you."

She nodded, turning to Butch. "You caught me?"

"Yeah, I did. I wish we'd met under different circumstances." Butch took her hand, kissing her knuckles.

"Eat," Zero said, standing on the other side of her, giving her a stern look. She rolled her eyes but picked up her spoon to start eating the slop. He hoped it was porridge.

"Zero has told us what happened last night," Tiny said, stepping at the foot of the bed.

Prue tensed and paused in eating. "Yes, Alan was here last night. He's a dangerous man and intent on hurting Zero any way he can." He watched her swallow the food, then wipe her mouth. "I'm done." She pushed the tray of food away from her.

"You need to eat more," he said.

"You try eating remembering how easily Alan got to me last night. From the way he spoke, he walked right past your man and no one even noticed him." She stopped, tucking some hair behind her ear. "He's dangerous, Zero. You should be taking care of your club as well. No one is safe."

"This is one man we're talking about," Tiny said.

"So, he's one man who has a serious fucking issue with Zero. This is a game to him. Alan is responsible for killing my brother, but he is the reason Alan is so angry." Prue pointed at him. "Alan will hurt whoever Zero cares about. This is only the beginning. He's got plans."

"Honey, he's not going to get to us," Butch said.

He watched her shake her head. "You'll be a fool to not take any warning. Alan will hurt anyone."

"Why didn't he kill you?" Steven asked, drawing the attention to him.

Prue paused, glancing at the younger man. "This is a game to him. It's what Alan said. He decided I would be much more fun to use. I was a messenger to let Zero know the games had begun."

Zero glanced at his brothers knowing they were thinking about what she said.

"There will be 'round the clock protection for you, honey. My wife will be stopping by to get to know you as well. You'll be getting a lot better than this shit grub," he said.

"Thank you." She smiled at Tiny, the sweet smile

Zero always loved to see.

"Zero, follow us out. Steven, stay behind and keep her company."

Wishing he could argue, Zero kissed her on the head then followed the rest of his brothers outside. His president pulled out a cigarette, lit it, and blew the smoke up in the air.

"She's fucking terrified," he said.

"Yes. I don't blame her. Alan got past Blaine. The nurses didn't even catch him. No one knew what the hell was going on until she started screaming." Zero grabbed his own cigarette, needing the relaxing quality of the nicotine. The last twenty-four hours had him on fucking edge.

"She's not leaving Fort Wills," Tiny said.

"I wouldn't leave her alone. I certainly don't want that fucker in there looking after her. I saw the way he was looking at her. Bastard needs to know to keep his eyes to his fucking self," Zero said, cursing. No one was taking Prue away from him. Not Steven either. Fucker screwed everything that walked, and he wasn't going to deal with that kind of shit.

What about Sophia?

Gritting his teeth, he saw the others were staring at him as if he'd gone mad. Maybe he had gone mad. Jealousy clawed at him, making his cigarette taste bitter.

"I'm sure Nash will appreciate the break of having to keep his woman," Butch said, smirking.

He hadn't seen Sophia since he'd tried to kiss her the night before. An apology was in order. One he wasn't looking forward to making, especially when he wasn't sorry at all. Only when he thought about Prue did he feel sorry for his attempts to kiss Sophia.

"You're coming home. We're leaving Steven to take care of Prue while you do. We need to get the others up to date. Whizz can do his thing on the computer. I'm not letting anyone get killed this time," Tiny said. "Too much fucking death going around. I fucking hate it."

Zero moved back to the hospital.

"Where the fuck are you going?" Tiny asked.

"To say goodbye to her."

Tiny shook his head. "Nice fucking try. I'm leaving Steven in charge. Butch just texted him to give him an update. Get on your bike, and get back to the clubhouse."

Wanting to argue, Zero fisted his hands and made his way back to his bike. His body ached from the beating he had taken and given out the other night. Killer hit the hardest while Nash stayed away from him. He imagined if Nash knew what he'd tried to do the other man would fuck him over.

Riding back to the clubhouse was uneventful. There were cars in the lot and several of the club hanging around their bikes, talking. He spotted the sweet-butts trying to get some action. Eva was at the side of the clubhouse where they'd installed a small park for the kids to play on.

Entering the clubhouse he walked up to his room and came up short as Sophia was sitting beside his door. Her knees were drawn up against her chest as she rocked to whatever beat she was listening to. Stepping beside her, he waited for her to get up.

She tugged the ear buds out, getting to her feet.

"What are you doing here?" he asked. She was a beautiful woman.

She's not yours.

For some reason the words didn't affect him. Staring into her eyes, he knew she wasn't ever going to be his, and for once he accepted it.

"Nash told me you were on your way back." She

looked down at her feet.

Reaching out, he tilted her head back, looking into her eyes. Sophia went tense but didn't pull away. "Why are you here?"

"You tried to kiss me last night," she said, biting her lip.

"If it wasn't for the gunshots I would have." He ran his thumb along her bottom lip.

Sophia drew away from him. "I love Nash. I will always love Nash."

"I know that."

She finally looked up at him. "He told me you've got a thing. Nash told me to be careful around you. I stay away, but you're always there. I'm not trying to hurt you. You're a nice man, Zero, but you're not the man I want. I care about you like a friend. Your touch, however, does nothing for me." She pressed a hand to her heart. "I can never be *in love* with you. Nash owns my heart."

Each word she spoke hurt, but it didn't feel like the end of the world. Prue's face entered his mind, calming him.

"You don't need to say anything more," he said.

"No, I need to. This is never going to happen. I love Nash. I'm the mother of his daughter." She pressed a hand to her stomach. "I'm going to be giving him another child very soon." He watched her swallow, tears in her eyes. "Find the woman meant for you. Don't wait for me. Stop wanting me. I'm never going to be yours to have."

She took another step back.

"I will," he said.

"Good." She took several steps away, turned around and left him alone.

Entering his room he saw Nash was sitting on his bed. "What the fuck do you want?" Zero asked. "Your woman has just told me how it's going to be."

"Are you going to listen this time?" Nash asked. He looked hurt, depressed even.

"Yeah, I'll listen. Sophia is in love with you, and I shouldn't have tried to think of having anything more. I'm sorry." He tugged his jacket off throwing it on the nearest chair.

"I've watched you for a long time. I know you want her, and denying yourself must be fucking hard. I know I wanted her for a long time before I took her," Nash said.

"Look, you don't need to do—"

Nash wouldn't let him finish.

"Sophia is mine. You tried to kiss her last night, and I heard what you said. You would have succeeded in kissing her." Nash stood. "I've fucked up in the past, but that gives you no right to try and steal my woman. While we were in Piston County Sophia and I talked about you. She promised she wasn't trying to lure you in or give you the wrong impression." Nash stopped, laughing. "She really thought you were friends. She didn't see your desire or what you wanted to do to her." Zero was slammed against the wall with Nash's arm over his windpipe. "I will not lose her to you. Get over your fucking crush, and get over her. She's not leaving me, and I won't let her leave."

He didn't fight Nash's hold. Zero knew he crossed the line, and if anyone tried to do this with his woman, he'd have flipped long ago. Nash had shown a great deal of patience and restraint.

"Next time I won't hold myself away from the fight," Nash said, referring to the night before when Zero needed to rid himself of the anger. "It will be you and me."

"I get it. Do you want to cut my junk off as

well?" Zero asked. "I've got shit to do, and this is boring me."

Nash jerked back then slammed his fist into Zero's jaw. Collapsing on the ground he heard the other man leave his bedroom.

Without saying a word, Zero stayed on the floor until he could focus on something. When he could, he got to his feet and walked into the bathroom. He was going to have a nice bruise on his face in the next few hours.

****

Steven was sweet. He didn't know what to say, and the conversation tended to be about nothing at all. They talked about everything and nothing.

"Have you never talked to a woman before?" she asked, smiling. Prue was charmed by his attempt to keep her company. Within a few minutes of being alone with him, she'd relaxed. He didn't scare her, which made a change from how she'd been feeling recently.

"Erm, talking is never really been necessary. I mean, I've talked to Angel and Tate, but they're, erm, they're taken. Other women, they're not hard, and conversation is the last thing on our minds."

Giggling, Prue grabbed her water and sucked on the straw. The blonde nurse hadn't made an appearance into the room yet, surprising Prue. She'd expected the other woman to be all over The Skulls, even Steven.

"They're women you've got no chance of fucking?" she asked.

"For a woman your language isn't all that great." He sat on the chair beside her bed.

"I grew up with my brother and Zero. He's not changed since joining The Skulls. Zero has always had vulgar language, and I picked it up from him." She sipped more water, smiling at the other man.

"He's never spoken of you."

"I don't expect him to. We're friends, but we don't have an impact on our lives. He came to me when he needs help or if it's a certain time." Zero hadn't visited her the last time she'd taken the time to remember Trevor. For the first couple of years after Trevor's death, Zero was always there. All of a sudden he stopped turning up, making excuses. Putting her glass down, she stared at him. "What about you? Any woman on the horizon?"

"No, no woman. I like to take what I like. There's something about variety I love."

He was blushing, and Prue couldn't help but laugh.

"It's charming seeing a man who blushes easily. How did you survive being a prospect?" Prue asked. "I'm sure they gave you more than your fair share of embarrassing jobs."

"I did just fine."

"I'm sure you did." She smoothed out the blanket covering her legs.

"You're not freaking out," he said.

"About what?" She tucked some hair behind her ear, looking at him. Steven was a handsome man. He was younger than Zero, possibly younger than she was. She was twenty-nine years old and been through her fair share of pain.

"Getting shot. I imagined you'd be freaking out."

She touched the cover that hid her scar. There were stitches binding her skin together. "I grew up with a brother who was always hurting himself. He actually shot himself in the leg." She chuckled, remembering the anger their parents had at Trevor hurting himself. Hanging out with two boys intent on adventure, Prue had ended up in all kinds of scrapes and accidents because of the boys' dares. "I don't know. I'm happy to be alive, and I've got company. It's nice not to worry. I'd be freaking out if I was alone. I'm pretending to be a big girl." Prue rarely lost control. Looking after young children who fell down and scraped their knees had trained her not to freak out at the littlest thing.

"You've been shot."

"It's not the first time I've seen someone shot. I was there when Trevor got shot. He didn't aim properly and was pissing about with a gun thinking he was some hotshot. Zero had to carry him all the way home, and I applied pressure to his leg. My brother squealed like a girl as if he was dying or something. We were all friends growing up. Trevor, Zero, and me. They didn't mind me hanging out with them, strange I know." She'd been a tomboy, rarely wearing dresses and preferring jeans to skirts.

"Your parents are dead?"

"Yeah, I'm the only one left of my family." She smiled even though she didn't feel like smiling. "Zero was part of our family, but he's not a blood relative. We're just friends." Prue was pleased. Her thoughts had nothing to do with brotherly love when it came to him.

"I'm sorry. I'm usually better at conversation."

"Yes, he really is," a woman said, entering the room. Glancing up, Prue saw a beautiful woman carrying a basket with a child on her hip. "Hey, honey, I'm Eva, Tiny's wife. I've come to say hi and to give you something a lot nicer than the hospital crap they serve up. I should know, there have been too many visits to this place. We should demand a refurbishment if we end up here again. I for one am getting tired of the stained walls. This is my daughter. Her twin brother is with his father." The basket was placed on the floor as Eva embraced her.

"It's lovely to meet you," Prue said.

"She won't let you starve," Steven said. "She's an amazing cook. All of us at the club are grateful for her skills. She left us once for a few weeks, and I had the shits for ages."

Eva clocked Steven around the head. "Don't talk like that." Steven laughed, rubbing at the part Eva hit. The basket was brought to the bed as her daughter sat on the bed "You don't mind Joanne being there, do you?" Eva asked, pointing at her daughter.

"No, I don't mind. It's fine." She smiled down at the girl then returned her gaze to Eva.

"Right, I've got enough food to sink a ship," Eva said, passing her a clear tub with a large sandwich. "Get dug in. Here you go, Steven. I brought you food as well."

For the next twenty minutes, Prue forgot about everything as she listened to the people around her. She ate the food given to her and smiled as Eva talked about family life and Zero. The club was a family, she soon realized. They were all there for each other, and if they didn't accept it they had to leave. Prue felt relieved that Zero had found people who took care of him. The thought of him being alone scared her. Losing Trevor had hit the other man hard, and she'd noticed the change within him the moment he collected her. Eating the food, she watched as a woman with long blonde hair entered. A large man covered with ink stood behind her, and his hand was on her shoulder, holding her close. On her hip was a boy. The woman looked like an angel. Her face was so beautiful, innocent almost.

Looking at them, Prue saw how protective the man was over his woman.

"That's Lash and Angel," Eva said. "With their young son."

"Hello," Angel said. She held up a sack. "I brought some clothes for when it's time to take you home. I didn't know what size you were going to need, but I also brought a belt in case they're too big."

Lash leaned down whispering to her. Angel blushed and glanced at the floor. "Sorry about that. I hate it when she puts herself down," Lash said, entering the room. "We thought we'd come and see Zero's little secret."

Laughing, Prue glanced at all of them. "Are you sure you're a biker club? You don't look all that scary to me." She smiled at each of them feeling part of their world. Since Trevor was taken from her, she'd been fighting every step of the way to make her life work. Teaching stopped her from being lonely, but when the nights came, she was always lonely. There was only so much lonely a woman could take.

"You've not been on our bad side," Lash said, holding onto his woman. "Wait until you piss us off, and then we'll terrify you."

The banter went around the room, and she settled back, enjoying the show.

Another two people entered. This time the man was larger than Lash and the woman fuller than Angel. "This is Killer and Kelsey. They're expecting their first child and have not long been married," Eva said.

Nodding at them, Prue was embraced by Kelsey. "You're part of the family now," Kelsey said.

"I doubt Zero will want me interrupting your time."

"You're not going home," Killer said. "You'll be part of the club for a while, at least until this fucker is caught."

Once again she watched them all. Steven drew her into a conversation. She answered his questions. Prue didn't know how much time had passed. Someone clearing his throat brought her attention toward the door.

Zero and Tiny stood in the doorway. Smiling at them, she watched Tiny go to Eva and tug her close. The chemistry she saw between the couple made her heart pound. What would it be like to be part of such need? She'd fucked, sure, but never had she experienced such heart-stopping passion.

Glancing at Zero, she saw he was staring at her.

"You look clean," she said.

He chuckled, moving toward her side. She looked up as he landed a kiss to her cheek. "I had a shower." The whole room was watching her.

She felt her cheeks heat at having an audience. "It's about time."

Zero stepped away, and the talking resumed. Steven stood, giving Zero his chair. She frowned as there seemed to be a silent message passed between the two people. The other man excused himself leaving the room. Frowning, she looked at Zero, who had a smirk on his face.

"What the fuck did you say to him?" she asked, glaring at Zero.

"Nothing."

"Don't give me that. I know you, Lucas Blakely. You and Trevor used to do the same kind of shit. What did you do?"

"Nothing." He held his hands up in the air.

She knew they had all of the others' attention on them. Prue didn't care. She'd never been afraid of giving Zero a piece of her mind.

"Steven has been nice to me. Don't think to throw your weight around or do some dominant man bullshit on him." Prue pointed her finger at him. "I know your game, don't."

"I'm protecting you," Zero said.

"You're protecting me from a weirdo you

created, not from Steven." She folded her arms underneath her breasts, glaring at the other man. "He's been nice and doesn't deserve you being a bastard to him."

"Fine." Zero glared back at her.

She heard the snickers around the room.

"I like her," Tiny said. "It's about time someone put him on his toes and bossed him around a little bit. It'll save us a job."

Zero raised an eyebrow at her, smiling. "She's the only woman I'll ever let talk to me like that."

"You couldn't stop me even if you tried. I'd kick your ass," she said.

"Remember who taught you how to hit. I let you win."

"In your dreams, asshole." Prue remembered Zero spending his afternoons teaching her how to defend herself. In school some of the guys had taken pleasure in bullying her over her weight and the fact she had large boobs. Prue hated it and refused to let her parents get involved. She could fight her own battles and often did. Zero wouldn't let her out in the world. Between him and Trevor, she learned how to hit back. Once she started defending herself, the bullies backed away.

"We'll see." He leaned, over ruffling her hair, and she slapped his hand away.

"Stop it."

She stared at him as the others started to talk. Zero was smiling at her, and when she felt heat pool between her thighs, she was so shocked that she turned her attention back to Eva. No, she wasn't going to let her feelings go there. Zero was her friend. He would never be a man in her life.

Staring down at her lap, she felt his gaze on her, and her nipples tingled in awareness. She would fight every response her body demanded.

****

"Please, let me go. I won't say anything. Please." The woman begged and pleaded for her life. Alan had her tied to a cross in the center of the forbidden warehouse. The economic downturn was good for something as it created available buildings for him to do whatever the fuck he liked to do. Staring around the room he listened to the woman snivel. He hated the sound of females moaning, begging. They were all whores, and he was tired of dealing with the low-lifes of this world.

Picking up the chef's knife, he'd sharpened it with a knife-sharpener, making it a deadly weapon. It was amazing how many weapons people could buy in any ordinary shop.

"You fucked Zero from The Skulls?" he asked, keeping his back to the woman.

She whimpered.

"I suggest you answer me or I'll make it far harder than it needs to be." He held the knife up to the light.

"Yes, I was with him."

"You fucked him?"

"Yes, I fucked him."

Alan smiled. He always loved the power he held getting what he wanted. Looking in the far corner of the warehouse he thought about the woman who'd pulled him out of the burning building ten years ago. He'd treated her like the treasure she was, taking care of her until she died a year ago. Clara hadn't been a whore. She'd been a good girl, a good woman, unlike this piece of trash in front of him.

Through his recuperation, the surgeries, the physiotherapy, Clara had been the only one by his side.

When she died, he buried her and then set about taking back what was his. Clara didn't care about his face or the damage done to him. It was a good thing Clara couldn't see him now. She didn't think getting his revenge was worth it.

Alan had nothing else to live for. The woman he loved was dead, and he had a select few men who stood by his side. By the time they were done, he was going to have everything back. Zero had taught him something ten years ago. He knew the other man had no intention of walking away and was prepared to die. There was nothing left for Alan. This game was going to be fun, and if he was lucky, by the end of their time, he was going to be dead along with Zero. Touching his face acted as a reminder to Alan. Zero was the first man to make him beg for mercy. The game was turned. Alan wasn't going to make Zero beg. He was going to make the bastard suffer, picking off the others around him before finally taking out the man himself.

He nodded to one of the men, who moved toward the bound woman, the nurse he'd taken from the hospital. Alan had a lot of eyes and ears. He looked forward to taking his time with this game, taking out everyone near Zero before finally killing him, himself. When Alan couldn't get around, he paid people to do his work. There was always someone willing to do something for money.

Thinking about Prue, Alan smiled. She was going to be so sweet to finally break. The love between the two was strong. He'd seen the way Zero was with her, and it wouldn't be long before he destroyed the pair of them.

The sound of fabric tearing and a feminine scream filled the air.

Turning toward the woman, the whore, the slut, he pressed the blade to her skin. Alan didn't care anymore about the blood. Revenge would be sweet.

"I better warn you, whore, you will die here," Alan said. "It's nothing personal. You shouldn't have touched Zero." He pressed the blade against her skin and slid it downwards. Yes, the game was truly in motion.

Chapter Four

Zero stayed behind as the rest of the men left for the day. Running a hand over his face he looked at Prue, who was working over a puzzle. She'd got on with Eva and the others as if they were old family friends. Prue's smile and sweet charm had always been refreshing for him. There was nothing fake about her, and she never tried to manipulate him. He watched her take sips from her drink and tuck her hair behind her ear as she nibbled on her lip, thinking. All of her actions drew him in. He'd never watched a woman's actions before.

"Why do you keep staring?" she asked, glancing over at him.

"I don't know. I'm pleased you're alive."

She smiled, sticking her tongue out at him. "I'm indestructible. You can't kill me. I'm like a superhero or something."

"You could have died, Prue. It's not a laughing matter."

"You're going to be miserable, aren't you?" She placed the magazine in front of her, dropping the pen on top of the machine.

"I'm being serious, and you could have died." If the bullet had been an inch down he wouldn't be sitting here talking to her. Losing her was not an option.

"Who gave you the shiner?" she asked, changing the subject.

"I deserved it."

"Who gave it to you?" She gave him a pointed look. Growling at her, he stood up moving toward the window in her room.

"Nash gave it to me."

"Great, I'll remember the name. He can kick your ass for me."

He turned toward her.

"Why did he hit you?"

"I've had a thing for his wife, and I about kissed her. I shouldn't have gone anywhere near her, but I never listen to reason and so he hit me." He shrugged. Sophia's words had hit him square in the face. Nothing he ever did would make her go for him. She was in love with Nash, not him. Zero expected pain, but there was none.

"I'm sorry. What was all that about Steven?"

"Fucker is into you," Zero said, feeling jealous of the younger man.

"So?"

"You want to be another whore in a whole line of them for Steven?" He folded his arms over his chest, facing her.

"I didn't say I was going to jump into bed with him. Fuck, what is with you?" she asked, glaring. "You're really bumming my mood at the moment. Do I need to kick your ass? Even being wounded I'd do it."

Visiting time was over, but Sandy had organized for him to be with her. Sandy was pulling a lot of strings with this hospital. He was sure they were looking for any excuse to fire her ass.

"Sorry, nothing is with me."

"You fuck everything that walks. One guy takes notice of me, and suddenly you're throwing your weight around as if you were my boyfriend or something. Newsflash, we're best friends."

Her words cut him deeper than Sophia's.

"I don't want you hurt."

"I've been hurt before, Zero. You were not there to mend my heart. In fact, the moment you're done with needing me, you're out the door," she said, folding her own arms underneath her breasts.

"That's not true."

"Yes, it is. The moment I didn't need you to keep the nightmares away you were gone like a shot. After Trevor died and we buried him, you were gone. When you were needed back home with The Skulls, you were gone." She named off every occasion he'd left her.

Whenever he was around her, he felt guilty.

It's not just that.

Being around her always made him want something he could never have. He'd promised Trevor he would take care of her. Wanting his deceased friend's sister was never going to happen. Prue knew him in ways other women would never get. She grew up with him and knew his parents didn't want him. No one ever wanted him. Gritting his teeth together, he took a seat beside her.

"You mean the world to me, Prue. Nothing is allowed to happen to you." He took her hand, but she pulled away from him.

"No, you don't get to hide from me."

"I don't want you with Steven." He yelled the words at her so she wouldn't have a doubt of what was going through his mind.

"Why not?" She yelled back, never taking his shit.

A nurse peered into the room ordering them to be silent. Going to the door, Zero closed it, giving them privacy, before going back to the bed.

"I don't want him near you. Please, do as I ask and don't push me."

She stared at him, collapsing against the bed. "You're going to drive me crazy with all of these demands." Prue grabbed the remote by the side of the bed, turning on the television.

"Is that a yes?"

"Steven is young, sweet even. I'm not going to be fucking the first guy who looks my way. I'm not that desperate," Prue said. "I know how to take care of my needs."

He tensed, thinking about her needs. "What?"

His cock tightened. How did she take care of those needs?

Crap. Now all he saw was her pussy. He didn't know what she looked like down there, but he suddenly really wanted to know. Zero would be more than happy to be considered to help her with those needs.

She's not yours.

Prue looked at him. "Are you a virgin?" she asked.

"No."

"Then you know what needs I'm talking about. Geez, you don't need to be a guy to need an orgasm or to get off." She shook her head, flicking through the television. "I'm usually looking over the kids' work now. How did the school take my absence?"

She was talking about work? All he could think about was taking care of her needs. "They want you to get well before you even think about returning to work."

"Good. I've never taken a sick day yet. They should keep my job for me. I'd hate to start looking now. The whole economic climate doesn't fill me with too much confidence on the job search."

"Have you ever thought about moving closer to me?" he asked.

"How would I do that when you said it wasn't safe for us to be close?" She turned to look at him. Her green eyes were so beautiful and wide.

"Alan's taken that out of our hands."

"Yeah, he has."

There was a game show on. He watched for several minutes, reaching out to take her hand.

"I've missed you, Prue."

"I've missed you, too." She rubbed at her temple, and he watched the movement. "Zero," she said, glancing at him.

"What, baby?"

"Will you hold me?" She tapped the bed beside her.

Smiling, he climbed on the bed, moving his arm underneath her head and drawing her close. "I'll always hold you close to me." They settled down together. He felt her heat, and his cock responded to her closeness.

Down, boy.

Her needs struck him once more. Would her pussy hair be the same as the hair on her head? *Shit.* Cravings yearned deep inside him. He wasn't some immature teenager who couldn't keep his dick in his pants.

"He's going to hurt us," she said.

"I know."

Zero knew there was not going to be a way to stop Alan once he started. None of them knew where he was. Whizz was working on locating him.

Closing his eyes, he tried to stop the fear from working inside him. He hated feeling fear.

"Your friends are nice. I would hate for them to be hurt."

He looked down at her. Her face was turned up to his. When did her lips get so plump and inviting?

Shit, this was the last thing he needed, for his mind to be on her body rather than the danger they were all about to face.

"We can't leave. Otherwise I would do it."

"Why can't we leave? When I'm out of the hospital we can just go." Her hand lay on his chest. Did she know what her body was doing to him?

"Alan will not stop, Prue. He's going to take out

our friends, and he'd do whatever he could to lure us
back to him."

"I hate him, Zero."

He didn't say anything. His feelings toward the
bastard had never changed. Alan needed to die, but until
they found him, they would have to play his games.

"Why did you do that to his face?" she asked. "I
know you said you tortured him, but why do that? Why
not just kill him?"

"I intended to kill him, Prue. It was never my
intention to let him walk free. I should have made sure he
was dead." His one biggest regret was walking away
without guaranteeing he was dead.

She settled next to him. "We've just got to wait?"

"Yes, we've got to wait."

Zero felt her relax, and he watched the television.
After an hour she finally settled into sleep. Assured she
was asleep he looked at her face. Her skin was pale, and
her complexion didn't have a single blemish. Reaching
out he cupped her cheek, stroking a thumb along her soft
skin.

"I'm always going to take care of you, Prue." He
kissed her cheek, feeling his cock pulse, demanding
attention. Watching the television, he was at peace.
Having Prue back in his arms settled something inside
him.

He wasn't yearning for Sophia or begging for a
fight. The beast he kept at bay was resting. The only time
he ever felt so calm was in Prue's arms. Ever since he
realized his parents despised him, Zero had always felt
some need to take out his aggression whenever he could.
Learning how to shoot helped him build his confidence.
The fights he got into were always worth the bruises. The
pain helped him to feel free all those years ago. That
feeling hadn't changed even now. The club fought him

when he needed it.

When Prue told him about the bullies all those years ago, he'd loved the hours he spent training her. She never acted like all of the other girls or women in his life. Prue treated him like a friend. She didn't blush or stutter in his presence, and she was never afraid to land him on his ass. When had he cut her out of his life? Over the years he'd tried to forget about her, only he found himself at her doorstep when he promised himself he wouldn't. Nothing had changed inside him. Prue was all grown up now, and they were both having to face their old enemy together.

Swallowing past the lump in his throat, he held her tighter knowing his life would be worse for losing her. She made living possible.

****

What the fuck am I doing here?

Butch sat in his seat at the back of the church. The candles were alight, and no one was around to see him. He looked at the man on the cross without feeling. There was no feeling inside him. Staring at the Bible, he wondered if he missed Cheryl. He asked Lash about her, but there was nothing his brother could say. Lash didn't remember anything about the other woman besides the fact she did beautiful flower arranging that Angel enjoyed looking at. It was like talking to a fucking brick wall.

"You're back," Cheryl said, holding a jacket in front of her. He noticed she had a bag on her shoulder.

Putting the Bible back in place, he stood. Her smile didn't waver, and neither did her gaze. She knew who he was, yet her gaze didn't leave his eyes. All of the women he'd been with checked out his cut before settling on him.

"Yeah, I'm back. I don't know why."

She smiled. "It doesn't matter why. Maybe you need some help in your life. Church is always open. I hope you find your answers soon." Cheryl took a step toward him. "Good night."

His heart raced as she stepped around him. She didn't try to rub against him.

"Where are you going?" he asked, not wanting her to leave. The only reason he'd come to church was to see her.

"I'm going home. It's late, and I only help out at the church when I can."

"Can I walk you to your car?"

"I don't own a car." She hadn't looked anywhere but at his eyes. This was an entirely new experience for him. Most of the women were after the title of fucking a Skull. Cheryl didn't look upset or expectant when she stared at him.

"How do you get home?"

"I walk." Cheryl chuckled and looked down at her feet. "Not all of us need a car or a bike to get us around."

"Are you teasing me?" he asked.

"Maybe. It's nice seeing you again, Butch."

He stood still watching her leave the church.

What the fuck are you doing? Follow her.

Walking out of the church, he shouted her name as he spotted her at the gate.

"You're acting strangely," she said, stopping at his call.

He felt like he was insane. Butch didn't want her to go.

"Can I walk you home?"

"It's perfectly safe for me to walk on my own."

"I want to walk you. I don't like the thought of you being alone."

She frowned. "I walk alone all the time. Fort Wills is safe."

"Not anymore, I don't want you walking alone." He stood close, and he got a hint of lemon. Was that her shampoo or soap? He knew he was really losing his mind. What was it about Cheryl that kept him wanting to come back to her?

Nothing made any sense to him anymore. The sweet-butts at the clubhouse didn't hold any appeal.

"How about I walk you home whenever you need it?" he asked. He looked forward to seeing her again.

"You're going to waste your time walking me home?"

"Why not? I've got nothing else to do."

"You're a strange man, Butch. I've got to stop off at my mother's," she said.

"Why?"

"I need to pick up my son."

Okay, something just hit him in the gut, and he felt the big man upstairs was laughing at him.

****

Prue was once again surrounded by warmth. She loved the heat, and opening her eyes she looked up at the ceiling. The television was playing to itself. Zero felt quite heavy against her. Looking around the room, something caught her eye at the bottom of the bed. Something red was there, facing them. Blood.

Screaming, Prue scrambled up waking Zero up in the process. A woman was tied to a chair that was next to the wall.

"Prue, what's the matter?" Zero asked, waking up.

She screamed again. The sight before her made her feel sick. "Please tell me this is some kind of joke. Is it real?"

Her heart was racing. The machines were beeping. The door to the room opened, and the nurse walked in. The moment the other woman walked in and saw the dead body, she screamed then fainted. Chaos ensued as the noise brought more people. Prue was getting tired of the screaming. The sight before her was making her feel sick. How had someone sneaked in a dead body?

Why hadn't anyone entered the room?

"Is it real?" she asked.

Zero moved closer. There was a knife in the center of the chest with a piece of paper plastered to the body. Without her glasses Prue couldn't read it. Zero flipped open his cell phone, pressing buttons madly. Prue couldn't believe what she was seeing.

"Tiny, yeah, you need to get to the hospital before the police do. Alan has struck again." Zero hung up the phone, sitting on the edge of the bed. He held onto her leg, and she felt him shaking.

"Do you know who it is?" she asked.

"Yes."

"Who is it? What does the note say?" Her hands were shaking. This was not what was supposed to happen. She was a teacher. Her life was not important. This kind of creepy shit was only supposed to happen in the movies.

"It's the blonde nurse I fucked the other day," he said.

Her face had been cut up, and from the stench, she'd been covered in petrol.

"What does the note say?" Prue asked, not really wanting to know the truth.

Zero hung his head. "I fucked Zero, and he cannot save me. Every person connected to him will suffer worse than the next. I'm disgusting and need to be reborn. Set me on fire, and see if I rise like a phoenix or die like the next person. I was once a nurse, and now I'm nothing. Come on, Zero, come and play. By the time I'm done there will be zero people you care about. One by one I will pick them off. Come out and play."

Prue felt sick. "Alan did this."

Zero leaned down, picking up a syringe. "Yeah, he did this, and he wants us to know how easy it is for him to play us like this."

"What's with the syringe?" she asked.

"He drugged us with a fucking sedative. Fuck, I woke last night when I felt a sting in my arm, but I didn't see anything, and then I couldn't keep my eyes open. He must have done the same to you only put it in your medication to be fed into you. I bet this is sedative to keep me knocked out. You know we're not heavy sleepers. We would have heard him enter and do this. Fuck, he knows someone at the hospital. He has to. It's the only way to get help."

Prue pulled the blanket up close. "No one is safe, Zero, and you can't just go around accusing people."

"I know."

She stared at Zero without knowing what to say to comfort him. It would have been better if Zero had made sure Alan was dead ten years ago.

"He's going to hurt everyone."

"And make sure I know what he's doing every step of the way." Zero moved up beside her. "Everyone has to be careful, and so do you. He will come after all of us at some point. I'm not going to make it easy for him. I refuse to."

"We can't always be on watch." She tried to reason with him. Zero wasn't having any of it.

"The cops are going to want to question me," Zero said.

"What? Why?"

"My name is on this letter. They'd be assholes not to question all leads, including people she fucked. I was one of them in the last few days."

Prue whimpered. This was getting worse by the second.

Tiny entered the room twenty minutes later followed by Butch. It was only a matter of time before the police arrived. She knew they were not happy at the sight of the dead nurse.

"They're going to ask you questions, Zero. You're going to need to go with them," Tiny said. "Another death in Fort Wills. There's only so much the law will take, and your name is plastered to the fucking body. You're the one they're going to want to speak to first."

"Then get the lawyer on the phone. I'm not going down for fucking a woman, and I won't have anything to do with this. I don't deal with the fucking police. One of our guys went with the police, helping them, and he got put away for it. He's still in fucking jail for *helping* the police."

She rubbed at her neck, hating how easily he spoke of the woman who was dead.

"She didn't deserve to die," Prue said.

All the men turned to look at her.

"We know." Tiny rubbed a finger over his lip. "Okay. I'm calling Devil. We're going to need his help."

"You can't bring that maniac here," Zero said.

"I'm calling him ready for help. I'm going to give him the heads-up. We don't know how far this fucker is going to go. He's a criminal and could have a shitload of backing. You didn't want to deal with this, then you should have put him in the ground ten fucking years ago," Tiny said.

"He was supposed to die in the burning fucking building. I fucked up. I know this."

"You branched out ten years ago." Tiny stepped closer invading Zero's space. She tensed. The older man looked like he could squash Zero without any effort. "Not once did you ask for club help, but now we're all involved. This is our fucking business."

"No, you're not. He's after me."

"He's going after everyone close to you. That means the whole fucking club. Angel, Lash, Nash, my kids and my woman, Sophia. Think about it, Zero. We're going to need all the fucking help we can get."

Tiny made sense. Alan wasn't going to stop until Zero begged for death.

"Don't argue," Prue said, speaking up. "You know he's right, Zero. We don't know where he is. This is a message. No one is safe, and you also know something else." She turned away from the remains of the nurse. If they didn't move her soon she was going to throw up.

"What's that?" Zero asked, going to her side.

"He's not planning on living. You once told me, in drink, how you got to Alan and what you did. You didn't care if you lived or died. There was nothing else for you. I was safe. This is what you did to him, but he hasn't burned her. Alan has nothing to lose. He's more dangerous than ever before."

"She's right," Tiny said.

Before she could say anything more the police entered the room. They saw Zero next to the body, and he raised his hands. "I've got to take you in, Zero. We got a call about you an hour ago, and we need to take you in for questioning," the officer said.

"I'm not going with you. I didn't do this," Zero said, folding his arms, facing off with the men.

"Zero, be reasonable. Go and give them a statement. Don't make this harder on everyone," Tiny said. "He's willing to give a statement, right?"

The officer nodded and put the cuffs away.

"We're not here to take you in, Zero. We want to ask you some questions about this. There was a phone call earlier speaking of you and this woman fucking. I need to ask you questions, get a statement from you, and then we can handle this."

She saw the determination on Zero's face. He wasn't going to be forced into anything. "Zero, don't do this," she said, begging him.

"I want a guard posted on her door. I can't leave her alone. You know what this lunatic is all about," Zero said, looking toward Tiny.

"After this incident I've already got a man posted on the door. He will follow her whenever she goes. Nothing will happen to her, I promise."

Zero was silent for many minutes, and no one spoke as he weighed up the problems. Prue knew what was wrong with him. Ever since they were young he'd always had a problem with being in tight, confined spaces. Something happened with his father where he kept him in a cage over a weekend or something like that. When he got out, he spent the week with her and Trevor at their house.

"I'm not doing shit. I fucked the woman, but I didn't fucking kill her."

"I'm not saying that you did, Zero. I'm offering my help as an officer of the law," the policeman said. "I can only do my job if you give me all the facts."

Zero shook his head. "No, you've got no way of dealing with this shit. You don't have the first clue what to do to help us. You can't even handle the fucking town. We're the ones who do it."

"Zero!" Tiny yelled. He wasn't listening.

She squealed as Zero lashed out, hitting the man who'd been talking. In the sudden chaos Zero was tackled to the floor, cuffed, and escorted out. The other Skulls were on the phone as they were also taken out of the room. Tiny was cursing and looking deadly as he followed them out. In the ensuing commotion she was tugged out of the bedroom and moved to a different ward. She heard Zero screaming about not leaving her alone. Panicking, she looked around the new room wishing there was something she could do. It was daylight, so no one could come to her.

What was happening to Zero? Why did he do that? All he needed to do was go with the police and give a statement. Now they could make his life a hell of a lot more difficult.

How did Alan manage to bring a dead body into the room?

The sound of the toilet flushing to her left drew her attention. She jerked as the man in question walked out of the room. He wore a jacket with a hood, hiding his face.

"What are you doing here?" she asked, terrified. Who had wheeled her bed into this room? What the hell was happening?

There was no Skull around, and the hospital staff was dealing with the dead body. She was all alone with a lunatic, a murdering lunatic.

He closed the door, flicking the lock. Next he drew the blind down before standing at the base of the bed. She gasped as he pulled the hood back, revealing his face. Prue stared into his eyes. They were dead of all emotion.

"Did you miss me?"

She pressed the emergency button. There was no

light beside her.

"This is an awful hospital. A dead body and they stop plugging in the electrics when they move you from room to room. Someone should complain about the standards in this shitty little town. You can shout if you want. I doubt they'll hear you over the yelling," Alan said. "Half of the cameras are fake. Did you know that? The security is around ten fat guards and a few cameras. Most of them are posted near the kiddie wards. They're more worried about the little ones than the adults," Alan said, grabbing her feet.

She whimpered at his touch. "What do you want?" she asked.

"I'm letting you know how easy it is for me to get to you. No one will stop me, Prue. Are you scared?"

"Terrified." Tears filled her eyes, and she gripped the sheet over her lap. "Are you going to kill me now?"

"Why would I kill you?" he asked.

"You want Zero to suffer."

"And you think him finding your dead body will be enough to make him suffer?" He moved up the bed. His fingers caressed up her thigh. Alan's touch repulsed her. She tried to jerk her leg away, but he held her tighter, his nails sinking into her flesh.

"I mean nothing to him. He's in love with someone else," she said, biting her lip.

"Ah, the lovely Sophia. He fancies himself in love with the other woman, but he's not." Alan shook his head. "No, he's not in love with that bitch, but she'll be fun to hurt when the time is right."

"You're going to hurt everyone?"

"Why, yes. If I didn't hurt everyone, I wouldn't be having any fun." His fingers grazed over her stomach.

Fear unlike anything she had ever known gripped her, threatening to consume her in the heat.

"Such a pretty sight. I love seeing a woman all scared. The blonde whore was scared until I snuffed the life out of her. Probably did the whore some good."

"Why did you kill her? She meant nothing to Zero." She bit her lip trying hard to contain the scream she wanted to let out.

"But she fucked him. You're going to realize, sweet Prue, no one is safe. I'm going to hurt everyone who ever touched Zero. If that means a couple of people die, I really don't care." He cupped her cheek, caressing her flesh.

His touch repulsed her.

"You're a monster."

"Yet, you're still alive," he said, smiling. "I can't be that bad. You'd be dead otherwise."

"Only until you've finished with me. I'm not a fucking idiot. You'll kill me when you're ready."

"I know. When I was little I loved to play games. I wonder who will win this game." He took a step back. The commotion outside was lessening, and Alan was moving away, ready to disappear again. Where were The Skulls when she needed them? Zero was going to get his ass kicked when she saw him.

"Zero will kill you," she said, trying to make him stay. If she kept him here someone might find them and Alan would no longer be a problem.

"And he will die along with me."

Alan left, and Prue could do nothing but wait for one of Zero's men to come and get her. They were not in charge. Alan was in charge, and there was nothing either of them could do to save each other. They were all at the mercy of a maniac.

Chapter Five

The police dropped all charges of assault and finally decided to take Zero's statement after he apologized to the man he hit. The man suffered with a broken nose. Tiny put up the money for the hospital funds. The officers wanted to keep him for longer for the attack, but they had nothing. He'd fucked everything up by refusing to come down and make a statement. Running a hand down his face, Zero had fucked up again. By attacking the officer he'd given the cops the perfect reason to believe he was hiding something. Zero knew he shouldn't have hit the other man, but his temper had gotten the better of him. Leaving Prue hadn't been an option, even though they agreed to post a guard outside the door. Fucking the nurse didn't make him a killer, and he wouldn't go down for that shit. During his statement, the police made sure he was aware that they were not here to pin the murder of the woman on him but were in fact asking him questions about the person responsible for killing the woman.

They treated him like a dumb fuck, and like Tiny told him, he had to deal with it. Fuck, he remembered when his father punished him years ago for something he didn't do. Zero couldn't remember what he had supposedly done, but he recalled the punishment. His father locked him in the dog cage for the entire weekend without feeding him.

Cutting off the memory, Zero remembered it was the one and only time he'd ever been trapped in something. Being behind bars was not something he ever anticipated. He'd rather go on the run before he went to jail.

Thinking about his life outside he doubted Alan wanted him in prison for the game to play out. How much fun would life be if he was locked away? He spent over twenty-fours in the prison cell for his own fucking doing, but it hadn't been all bad apart from the fact he didn't get to see his woman. Twenty-four hours felt like forever to him with nothing to do but deal with his own fucking problems. Tiny and the rest of The Skulls found ways of getting messages to him. Steven was with Prue in the hospital, watching over her, which he didn't like.

Next time go to the station willingly, fucking asshole.

He also found out what happened during the chaos of the discovery of the dead body. Collecting his stuff from the reception desk, Zero was in no mood for jokes. He ignored the banter going on around him. They were all talking about their normal lives full of normal shit. Zero hadn't lived a normal life in such a long time. Heading outside, he felt the heat of approaching spring on his face. After not seeing it for twenty-four hours and having nothing but three walls and bars, Zero was appreciative of any scenery outside. At least he no longer had an issue with cages anymore.

Tiny was waiting in the car along with Eva and the twins. He climbed into the back seat glancing at the innocent lives beside him. Fuck, he should have made sure Alan was dead before he left ten years ago. No matter how hard he tried, Zero wasn't going to be able to change the past. At the time he'd liked the idea of the other man burning alive. He'd been away from The Skulls for an entire weekend. The longer he was away, the less chance he had of being part of the club. He hadn't watched the warehouse burn. Ten years ago he'd fucked up and fucked up bad.

"I want to go to the hospital," he said. The thought of seeing Prue kept him going.

"You're not going to the hospital."

"Who is looking after her?" he asked, fisting his hands.

"Steven and Blaine have been dealing with it. Butch stops by as well. She's a nice girl, cheery all things considered." Tiny was the one driving. Eva stayed silent, looking out of the window. "We're going on lockdown. I can't risk our club. When Prue gets out of the hospital Sandy will take care of her. I'm not risking anymore lives. I can't."

Zero couldn't argue. "I'm sorry."

"What?"

"I fucked up. I should have made sure Alan was dead. I fucked up."

"Yeah, you fucked up bad. Whizz is working on locating him. So far, it's hard to track a ghost." Tiny tapped his fingers on the steering wheel. "I called Devil. He and his crew will be on their way the moment we need them."

"You called them?"

"Chaos Bleeds will help us. They're our friends, and you're going to deal with it," Tiny said. Chaos Bleeds was an MC group worse than The Skulls. Devil, the president, helped The Skulls out a couple of times in the last couple of years, but they didn't have any rules. They took without thinking who they hurt.

"We don't need them," Zero said.

You do. How can you fight a ghost?

"Really? So you were awake when this fucker took the blonde nurse you fucked, tortured her, and then tied her to a fucking chair after plunging a needle to keep you out of it." Tiny glanced at the inside rear mirror. His anger was tangible in the small space of the car. Eva reached out to calm the kids, who were getting restless as their father lost his temper. "For fuck's sake, use your fucking head, you fucking asshole. You didn't finish the job ten years ago. We've got no choice but to bring our friends in. The next time I tell you to do something, you will fucking do it. When I say go and give a statement, you'll fucking go. If I tell you to piss on demand, you'll fucking do it."

Zero stayed silent. Everything Tiny said rang true. Zero, ten years ago, had fucked up and fucked up bad. There was no chance of getting away from it.

"We're taking you to the clubhouse to wash the stink of the cells off you. When you're done, we'll take you to the hospital. Between you and Prue, neither of you are leaving without a fucking escort."

"Stop swearing, honey. The kids don't like it," Eva said.

He watched as Tiny grabbed Eva's hand, locking their fingers together. The love and support was strong. Zero wanted something like that. The couple was strong together. They led The Skulls, drawing them all together as a family. They'd been married a couple of years, but Eva had been part of the club for a lot longer.

At the clubhouse he ignored all the stares that followed him. Going straight to his room, he found Butch waiting on his bed.

"Fuck, Nash the other day and now you. What the fuck?" Zero said, cursing.

"I wanted to make sure you're all right," Butch said. "I brought you into the club. I vouched for you even though I'd only been a full member for a few months. I like you, Zero. You're a good friend. You're loyal."

Butch had been a friend he made in a bar. Zero at the time had gone by Lucas, and he'd been working odd jobs, moving from place to place. He owned a bike, never stopping what he was doing. Everything was always brilliant and new to him. Settling down hadn't been in his blood. For several months after he met

Butch, he'd learned a little about the club life until he'd asked how to become part of it. Zero didn't regret being part of it. He loved his life and wouldn't change anything.

"I fucked up," Zero said. "There is nothing I can say to change that. I wish I'd come to the club, but I just acted. I got Prue safe, and then I needed justice for Trevor being dead." He gritted his teeth hating the pain that pounded through him.

"I met someone." Butch changed the conversation quickly.

Frowning, Zero didn't know where this was going. "Someone special?"

"Yeah."

"She's not a sweet-butt?" Zero asked.

"No, she's not a sweet-butt. I don't really know who she is. She has a son." Butch ran a hand down his face. "I don't know what this is." He placed a hand in front of his chest, looking confused.

"Why are you telling me?"

"I need to tell someone who knows all about being confused by their fucking feelings." Butch ran a hand down his chest.

"The sweet-butts will be so angry if they lose you," Zero said.

"Nothing is going to happen. I don't have anything to do with single moms." Butch stood up. "I'm pleased we had this chat."

Before Zero could say anything else, Butch was leaving his room. When did he become the person to talk to? He knew fuck all about love let alone showing a woman how he felt.

He went to the shower and took a quick wash. In ten minutes he was downstairs waiting for Tiny to come.

Running fingers through his hair, he waited

outside. Eva and Tiny were in his office, and it didn't take a genius to know what they were doing.

Sophia stood outside with her daughter. Nash was close to her, and she was looking after all the kids. He watched them for several minutes seeing the love shining between the couple. They were in love. Zero was an idiot to think she would ever have fallen for him. He had next to nothing to offer her.

Taking out a cigarette, he placed it to his lips and lit it.

"He'll get over it, you know," Lash said, coming to stand beside him. Lash was Nash's brother. The two were really close, and both were married with kids. For the first time, Zero was envious of the men settled down.

"What?"

"Your crush over Sophia. He can't blame you really. Nash claimed her for a reason." Lash leaned against the wall, watching his brother. "It's why I couldn't blame Devil for wanting my woman. Angel is everything to me. I wouldn't let anything happen to her."

Zero followed his gaze as he looked toward his woman, who was talking with one of the sweet-butts. Everyone knew not to upset Angel. Once Lash found out, you made an enemy.

"Angel is a beautiful woman. She's sweet." Too sweet for their life but Lash wanted her, and so they made it all possible.

"If anything ever happened to her it would kill me. She's my world. My life is devoted to the club. She never makes waves and never asks questions. Angel trusts me completely with her life and that of our son and future children when they come." Lash turned back to look at him. "I will not live without her. She's my lifeline and what makes me a good man."

"Why are you telling me this?" Zero asked.

"There is a woman lying in the hospital who means the exact same thing to you. The moment she was in danger you forgot about everything else to be with her."

"Prue's my friend."

"And yet, even for a friend you wouldn't be lying in a hospital bed, holding her tightly. I stopped by the night the nurse was found tied to the chair, though obviously before she was actually there. Tiny wants us all to keep an eye on you both. You were holding Prue tightly, Zero. I wanted to make sure you were all okay. Don't worry, I didn't stay around to watch you or shit. That's fucking creepy. You need to think about where your heart truly lies." Lash gave him a pointed look and then moved away.

Zero did love Prue. But his feelings didn't delve any deeper than friendship, or did they?

****

Steven was bloody awful at playing cards. Prue had won three rounds of snap, and he still couldn't grasp it. He took his time putting cards down and looked them over.

"You know, snap is the easiest game to play," she said, frowning at him. "How did you become part of The Skulls if you can't play snap?"

"I've never played it before. Also, I'm letting you win." He looked at her over the top of his cards.

Pursing her lips, she watched him slowly put down a five, and she picked the top of her cards putting down a king. They'd watched television for the better part of the morning. She couldn't believe the drama on the talk shows. It was overplayed and boring. Prue missed her school and the kids she taught.

Staying in bed all day was awful. She hated not being able to do anything. Her wounds were healing nicely, and there was no sign of infection. It would be a matter of days before she went home, which she was thankful for. Zero hadn't been gone for that long, but she missed him.

"This game sucks. It's boring."

"What do you want to play? Strip snap?" She rolled her eyes, chuckling. "Any news on Zero?" She knew he'd been put away for the last couple of days for being a fucking idiot.

"Tiny's picking him up this morning. They can't keep Zero when all of his alibis check out. Last time I checked even officers can't keep people for being irritating. There is footage of him entering the hospital as well. Some of the security cameras were working, but none of them worked after two o'clock. You've got an extra guard on the door, courtesy of the local law." Steven placed his cards down, refusing to pick them up. "This game sucks. I'm not playing."

"Fine. You're useless at it anyway." She settled back in the bed looking toward the window. "Have you been to the hospital often?"

Steven laughed. "Baby, we've lived in this fucking hospital the last couple of years. I'm surprised Tiny hasn't invested some capital into the place."

"Great, people with The Skulls are known to spend time in hospital. Great, I feel all happy knowing I'm being looked after."

He stopped smiling, and she shot him a glare, folding her arms underneath her breasts. She was so fucking bored.

"We take care of everyone, Prue. We can't fight everyone," Zero said.

She turned to look at him. He held a bouquet of white roses. They were her favorite.

"Are those for me?" she asked. Her heart lifted at

the beautiful sight.

"Nah, I brought them for Steven. I thought he could do with the pick-me-up after spending the past couple of days with you." Zero stepped into the room walking around to the other side of the bed. "Of course they're for you. I wouldn't forget what your favorite is." He placed them on the bed and kissed her cheek. "Sorry it has been a short time since we saw each other." He tucked some hair behind her ear.

Prue's heart flipped over at his closeness. They hadn't been apart for long, but it felt like a long time. She missed him so much when he was away. Most of the time she cut off her feelings not wanting to let herself think too deeply about what they all meant to her.

He withdrew, and she missed his closeness the moment it was gone.

"You can go," Zero said, looking past her to the younger man.

Seconds later they were alone. "I didn't think I was awful company."

She watched him take the flowers from her bed, place them beside her, and tug the blanket down her legs.

"Hey, what are you doing?" she asked.

"We're getting out of this fucking room. I've been locked up for the last couple of days. I'm not visiting you confined to the bed." He left the room and came back minutes later with a wheelchair.

"Do all of your women end up in the hospital at some time or another?" she asked, stepping off the bed. He wouldn't let her take another step. Zero lifted her up as if she weighed nothing. She wished it was true. Prue had always loved her food, and if she stayed with Eva, her size fourteen, occasional sixteen, was not going to last.

"We've been unlucky, but all of our women have

lived."

"I suppose that's good."

He stepped behind her and started wheeling her out of the room. Letting out a sigh, she relaxed into her seat, closing her eyes. This was what she'd been craving ever since she got here. Steven wouldn't let her leave the private bedroom even though the nurses advised it and believed it would do her good.

"I'm sorry I wasn't here for you. Tiny told me Alan visited again," Zero said, pulling her out of her carefree spirit.

"Yeah, he dropped by to show how powerful he was." She shivered from the fear clawing up her spine. What Alan wanted, Alan got. Nothing she or Zero did was going to stop him. "He waited ten years for this, and now he's going to have all the fun he can."

"My thoughts exactly. I've got one of the boys looking into him, seeing if he crops up anywhere."

"He's like a ghost. No one has seen him."

"You've seen him. Do you think you could draw him or at least describe him to someone who can draw?" Zero asked.

"Oh, like one of those crime photos. I've always wanted to do that."

"Stop kidding around."

Prue sighed, rubbing her temples. "If I don't kid around it makes being scared easier."

Zero stopped near a bench. He put the brake on her wheelchair and sat down in front of her. His hands rested on her knees. She felt the heat of his touch travel up her body. The delightful warmth spread through her pussy making her wet.

Cut these thoughts off.

Staring into his eyes, she wondered how she was going to survive the next couple of weeks with her heart intact. Since Trevor's death she'd only seen Zero a handful of days. Each day they stayed clear of one another. She cooked for him, clothed him, but they did nothing else. They were friends and treated each other as such.

"What's going to happen when I get out of hospital?" she asked, changing the subject. Talking about Alan wasn't going to make the other man disappear. He was the bogeyman that came out in the night. She hated horror stories and was currently living her own.

"You'll come to live in the clubhouse. Tiny is organizing a lockdown. Alan's threats are being taken seriously. We can't risk anything going wrong. The clubhouse and the compound is the safest place to be." Zero's hands started moving up and down her thighs.

Didn't he have a clue what his touch was doing to her? It was hard to concentrate when his touch took away the ability to think.

"All of us in one place, is that a good idea?"

"He can't pick us off one by one. All of us together are safer than alone. Alex, one of the guys, is flying to Vegas to talk to Eva's father. We band together like brothers, taking care of everyone and each other. You'll be safe there, and so will I." Zero gazed over her shoulder. "I put everyone in danger."

Prue didn't dispute him.

"I should have killed him back then."

"Instead you tortured the man, and now he's back intent on hurting everything you hold dear," she said. "Sorry, maybe you should have just killed him, not maimed him."

"I intended to kill him. I wanted to hurt him. I held Trevor as he died, and I wanted the bastard who killed him to know what true pain really felt like." Zero glared at his hands where they held her legs. "I made every second hurt. He screamed and even begged me to stop, but I didn't. I couldn't bring myself to show that kind of mercy."

Swallowing past the lump in her throat, Prue looked around the hospital grounds seeing the people coming and going. Their lives hadn't changed. They were all carrying on with the mundane tasks life throws at them. None of them knew what it meant to truly suffer or to beg. Alan was out there, watching, waiting. No one was going to rush him into anything. He would take his time until he was ready.

"He's waited ten years for this moment," she said, holding onto Zero's hands.

"I know."

"Ten years of waiting. Ten years of letting his hatred fester. Whatever he's going to do, it's not going to be pretty, Zero. He's going to make life hard and painful." Tears filled her eyes thinking about the blonde he'd killed. Yes, the blonde had fucked Zero, but no one deserved to die.

"I know." He gripped her hands, looking into her eyes. "I can't let anything happen to you, Prue. You mean the world to me."

She smiled. "I'm a lot stronger than I look."

"Not many women would be so calm after being shot at."

Prue shrugged. "What can I say? I'm perfect."

He chuckled. The sound was hollow, and the smile didn't reach his eyes. Leaning forward, she cupped his cheek.

"Hey, you made a mistake. It's in the past. It's all in the past, and there's nothing we can do about it." She dropped her gaze to his lips. Big mistake. She didn't want to be thinking about his lips or wondering what they would feel like on her body. "You cannot change what happened. Neither of us can. Trevor is gone, and he wouldn't blame you. He'd be pissed, but he wouldn't let you hurt yourself for what happened." Prue closed the distance, pressing her lips to his. The kiss was friendly, and she withdrew within seconds of their lips touching, trying to avoid the temptation to deepen the kiss. "I'm not going anywhere. We're in this together like we've always been."

She watched him rub the tears from his eyes. "Now I feel like a fucking pussy."

Prue chuckled. "You're not a pussy. You're not even close. We'll do this together. You've got the club, and you've got me." She tightened her hand around him.

If she was given the chance, she'd never let go.
****

"So, let's see," Alan said, spreading out the pictures on the floor. Zero was back in the game, thank fuck. Hurting him was going to be fucking hard in prison. He couldn't believe the bastard attacked a police officer and risked ruining his game. Alan would have no choice but to hurt the officer then for spoiling his fun. The Skulls had a lot more friends than they deserved.

Clicking his tongue he looked over the pictures as the three men who still served him played cards. He paid them plenty of money to remain loyal along with a couple of security guards in the hospital. It was amazing seeing what desperate men did when someone paid the right amount of money. "Angel, blonde haired bitch belongs to Lash." Alan matched the two pictures together. The couple looked happy. "It's a shame Lash has anything to do with Zero. It's going to be fun watching them die."

Next he aligned Eva with Tiny. They were going to be the hardest to kill. He didn't want that bastard Ned Walker trying to hurt him before he was done. If he survived killing Zero, he'd finish them off for fun, maybe take out Ned while he was at it. This was fun, such a fun, delightful game to play.

He picked up Sophia's picture. She was holding her daughter and standing next to Nash. "It's a shame Zero felt himself in love with you, honey. Poor you. I wonder how your slut of a daughter is going to feel without a mom."

One after the other he aligned up the picture of The Skulls with their women or left them bare. They all meant something to Zero, and that meant they all had to go.

Lockdown was going to happen. He had his sources, and it was fun being able to be overlooked. No one ever seemed to remember seeing a man with a hood sticking to the shadows. Alan couldn't believe how easy and how much fun it was getting around Fort Wills. Then he had people who gossiped. All he needed to do was listen and he found everything he needed without any problems.

Without anyone looking for him, the town was his oyster. His obsession was Zero, that one man. The one man who nearly killed him ten years ago. The very same man who scarred up his face making him look like a fucking monster. The one man who Alan was going to hurt and then kill, slowly, making every bone shatter.

Zero was going to know what true suffering really felt like before he died.

Chapter Six

A couple days later

Zero climbed out of the car leaving Steven behind the wheel as he made his way into the hospital. In the last couple of days there hadn't been a single sighting from Alan, and no one had turned up dead. Whizz was still checking shit out, and it was going to take some time. Locating a dead man was a lot harder than they realized. To the world, Alan was dead. No one knew where he had gone from that burning building ten years ago or where he was now. He didn't even have a picture of the bastard to help Whizz in his search.

The club was on lockdown, the women and children forced to live within the compounds grounds. It was a tight fit, but with everyone chipping in, life was actually quite fun. Zero enjoyed waking up to the sound of all the family around him, screaming kids and all. He wouldn't admit it to anyone, of course. That was his little secret to take with him to his grave.

He went straight to Prue's room. A doctor was talking to her about her medications. Leaning against the wall he watched her nod, tuck some hair behind her ear, and concentrate on everything the good doctor had to say.

When they were done, he passed the doctor going to her bedside. She wore a pair of jeans and a plain white shirt.

"Hey, you. I was worried you'd forget about me," she said, smiling.

Her bags were all packed, and she was no longer hooked up to several machines. She had pulled her red hair back in a ponytail leaving some wisps of hair to fall around her face. The clothes were a little large on her, but it all worked. She looked revitalized and fresh.

"How could I forget you? You nag me enough." He walked into the room, grabbing the bag from the bed. "Are you good to walk, or do you want me to grab a wheelchair?"

"Nah, I'm going to walk out of this hospital." She linked her arm through his, and together they made their way toward the car. Nurses stared at him, but Zero only had eyes for the woman by his side. He was going to make sure she walked out of the hospital the way she wanted.

Alan wasn't darkening their days here, and he wasn't going to let the other man's presence spoil this moment. He had Prue in his town and about to be inside his club. Zero knew once the men got to know her, they would fall for her. She was easy to like.

He kept her away all these years to protect her. Trevor always wanted her to finish school and have everything her heart desired.

"Oh, you brought the car to collect me?" she asked.

Steven was waiting with the door open. Blaine was in the passenger side, and Zero would be sitting beside her.

"This is such a bummer. I was hoping to have a ride on your bike." She smiled at him, shrugging her shoulders.

"Come on, stop trying to push your luck. You'll be riding a bike in no time. I know what you're like." Zero helped her inside the car, taking extra care to secure the seatbelt across her lap. He brushed across her breasts, and he pulled away before he was tempted to do something else.

Moving around to the other side, he climbed in, and Steven was driving away.

He grabbed her hand, locking their fingers together.

"Wow, you're all so morbid. Come on, we're all alive still. We'll get there. I know we will," Prue said.

The men slowly relaxed and were talking about football. Zero wasn't ready to start talking to the others. He wanted Prue all to himself. When they got to the clubhouse he'd have to fight to get her to himself. Eva liked her, and so did Angel and Kelsey. Prue hadn't met Tate yet.

Zero inwardly groaned thinking about the other woman. Tate was one of those women you either loved or hated. He was still on the fence of loving and hating her. She was Tiny's daughter, but apart from that, there was nothing special about her.

He hoped Tate didn't piss Prue off. She had grown up with him and Trevor, and not once did she learn how to keep her opinion to herself.

The drive went by quietly in the back with Blaine and Steve talking between themselves. The gate to the compound was being manned by Butch and Tiny, who opened the gate when they came into view.

"This is the security?" she asked.

"Yeah, everything is locked up. Alan will not be getting inside, and we also have plenty of security cameras in place." The car came to a stop, and he climbed out, going around to Prue to help her out.

She looked tired, and he wanted to make sure she got plenty of rest.

"Welcome to the clubhouse," Tiny said, pulling her in for a cuddle. She chuckled, wrapping her arms around the large man. Zero felt jealousy hit him square in the gut. What the hell was wrong with him? Tiny was taken and wouldn't want Prue.

The jealousy didn't stop as the men greeted her,

ZERO

either hugging her or kissing her hand. She was tugged into the main house where Eva took over, leading her around the group of women. Kids were running around, and babies were being held. The clubhouse was in total disarray. The sweet-butts were on their best behavior being forced to wear clothes that covered every inch of flesh. The men knew not to push their luck in trying to get them naked as well. Any kind of sex would be done behind closed doors, away from kids and family.

"So, you're Prue," Tate said, standing in front of his woman.

Zero fisted his hand at his side.

"And you are?" Prue asked.

"Tate, I'm Tiny's daughter, and Murphy's old lady."

Prue nodded. "Okay."

"What are your intentions?" Tate asked, stopping Prue from moving away.

"Excuse me?"

"We're all in lockdown because of you. I want to know what your game is." Tate was glaring at his woman.

Glancing around he saw Eva looked annoyed while Tiny was making his way toward them.

"Tate, baby, not here," Murphy said.

He saw her hesitate, but Prue finally spoke up.

"First of all, you're Tiny's daughter. Eva is his woman. She knows why I'm here. Both of them know why I'm here. You got a problem then take it up with them. If you still want to be a bitch, I'll show what it's like to take an ass whooping because I learned from the best." Prue took a step closer getting up close to Tate.

"Who did you learn from? I'm Tiny's daughter. He's the best."

"He's a leader, but I learned from an experienced

105

fighter. You want to fuck with me let's do this, but lose the kid. I don't fight mothers with kids on their hip." Prue wasn't backing down.

This was the first time a woman had stood up to Tate.

Tiny looked impressed. "Tate, honey, your ass has been handed to you. Back down, and her presence here has nothing to do with you. You're going to get along just fine." He tapped Prue on the back, and Tate backed down.

The two women stared at each other a long time.

"It's nice to meet you," Tate said.

"And you. I hope we can be friends." Prue shook Tate's hand before moving around. Zero introduced her to Rose and Hardy then to Blaine and his woman and kid. They were at the clubhouse over three hours before he finally got her to his room.

"Wow, you've inherited a lot of family."

"It's the club," he said, opening his door.

"They're your family. They all care about you. I think they're a little pissed at you for taking matters into your own hands." She shrugged, entering his bedroom behind him. "This is your room?"

"All the guys have their own room. The sweet-butts usually share, but when the family is in, they're sent to a section of the house away from the men. They do mingle when needed." Zero closed the door behind them. The temptation to lock the door was there, but he ignored it and watched her look around his room. She tugged the pants up, wriggling her ass. His gaze landed on her rounded curves.

"I can't believe you handed it to Tate. She's a bitch and puts a lot of people through their paces."

She moved toward the picture of the two of them with Trevor on top of his drawer. "She's used to being the alpha. I bet she's pissed at being in lockdown and all because of me. She doesn't know what's going on?"

"It's up to Tiny and Murphy to make her aware of what's going on."

Prue shrugged. "I would have whooped her ass if she didn't back down. I'm not going to have a bitch in my face. I didn't take it in school, and I'm not taking it now."

"You earned a lot of respect down there."

"Tate's a woman. I imagine Tiny won't let any guy hurt his little girl even if she does need it." She sat down on the edge of his bed. "This is a nice room. Don't you have a house or anything?"

"No, this is my home. I've never needed a house."

"Where will I sleep?" she asked.

Moving to sit beside her, Zero enjoyed the heat of her closeness. "We've shared a bed before. I really need to hold you right now, Prue. I need to know you're going to be okay."

"You presume too much. I'm not that easy." She nudged his shoulder, chuckling. "Of course I'm fine with it."

He followed the direction of her gaze. She was looking at the picture of the three of them.

"I really do miss him," she said.

"I do as well. It's not the same without him." Zero rubbed his hands together wanting more than anything to hold her close.

"What do you think he'd say to us now?" she asked, leaning back on the bed to look up at the ceiling. The way she lay exposed a strip of her stomach. Why did that strip of skin seem more tempting than anything else he had the pleasure of seeing?

"He'd be pissed at putting you in danger. Trevor

was a lot of things, but he loved you, Prue. He did everything he could to protect you."

He heard her sigh. Leaning back beside her, he was shocked when a few seconds passed and she curled up against him. "I wish he was here."

At that moment, Zero was really pleased he wasn't.

****

Later that night Prue sat around with the women of The Skulls, eating one of the nicest pies she'd ever tasted in her life. It was a meat filled pie, and she'd piled her plate high with mashed potatoes, vegetables, and drowned the plate with gravy. After the crap food at the hospital, she was starving.

She dove in as the men ate and drank, playing pool or shooting darts. Every time she looked toward Zero he was staring back at her. Each time she caught his gaze she felt an answering pulse between her thighs. What was going on?

"Zero keeps staring at you as if he wants to eat you," Sandy said, leaning in close to whisper against her ear.

"What?" She jerked away from the other woman. Zero wanted to eat her?

Looking toward him, he was talking with Steven. No, he didn't want to eat her. He was putting up with her because of Trevor.

"I've seen that look on Zero's face before. He's wondering what you look like naked."

"We're friends." Tucking some hair behind her ear, Prue continued to eat her food. Her appetite wasn't so ravenous anymore.

"He wants more."

She shook her head turning to Sandy. "No, he doesn't. We've been friends all of our lives. It's not going to change overnight."

"Maybe not tonight, but I bet you, you snuggle up close and you'll feel his need nestled against your ass." Sandy stood, going to the bar.

Prue watched the other woman pour herself a drink while talking with Stink. She saw the way the other man looked at Sandy.

"Sandy used to be a sweet-butt," Eva said, leaning in close.

"What?"

"She's fucked half of the club. Something happened a year ago, and she's now the club doctor and she doesn't need to put out for the men." Eva was eating from her own plate. Tiny took a seat beside her, wrapping his arm around his wife. "I'm eating here."

"Keep eating, baby. I'm not doing anything to stop you."

Eva rolled her eyes and finished off her plateful of food.

For the next hour Prue listened to the women talk. Kelsey was expecting her first child with Killer. It was early days, and the woman was nervous. Angel wanted another child, but Lash refused to put her through another birth yet. Tate remained silent throughout it all.

When she finished her dinner, Prue made her way into the kitchen. She wanted the silence and started washing the dishes.

"I want to know what's going on," Tate said, moving into the kitchen.

Letting out a sigh, Prue took her time cleaning the plates. Grabbing a towel, she dried her hands and turned toward Tate. When was this bitch going to learn to back the fuck down? "Why don't you ask your dad or even your man?"

"They're not telling me anything. I want to know

what's going on."

"You're used to getting what you want?" She knew their friendship was going to be stretched to the limit. Tate was a strong woman, but so was she. Their personalities were going to clash. Prue wondered how they were both going to get along. The other women clearly gave into Tate. She wasn't going to do it. Tate was going to learn the hard way.

"Yes." Tate pushed the word out through gritted teeth.

"I'm not part of the club, and I'm not going to piss men off because you want the truth. Ask them. Don't come to me." Prue folded her arms underneath her breasts, waiting for Tate to make the next move. It was like being back in the playground.

Murphy entered the room. "Go to our room, Tate," he said.

"You're keeping me in the dark." Tate turned to her man looking hurt.

"For once, realize I'm doing you a favor. Get to our room now."

She watched Tate hesitate. Finally, she turned away and left the room.

"If she caught Kelsey or Angel on their own she would know everything that's going on," Murphy said, shaking his head.

"Why are you keeping her in the dark?" Prue asked.

"There's shit she doesn't need to know. You're the first woman who has stood up to her. I appreciate it." He left the room.

Zero appeared next. His lifted his arms up holding onto the doorframe. "You turn me on talking shit to Tate."

Heat filled her cheeks. Laughing, she approached

ZERO

him. "I've got a lot more ways of turning men on." She
reached out touching his chest.

Something changed between them. The smile on
his lips dropped as did his gaze. He was looking at her
lips then at her breasts.

"I'm calling it a night," she said, brushing past
him. He caught her arm, and she looked down at the
floor. Not tonight, she couldn't handle this change
tonight. Listening to the women talk and have them tell
all secrets she knew he had a thing for Sophia.

"Don't go." He didn't pull her arm closer.
This is your choice.
Sandy's words came back to her.

No, she wasn't going to be a means to an end. If
Zero wanted her then it was going to take some time. She
wouldn't be second best for any man.

Pulling on her arm, she took several steps away.
"Good night."

She left him alone, making her way upstairs to
their room. Closing the door, she leaned heavily against
it. Her heart was racing, and her pussy was on fire,
burning with need.

Think about Alan.

This was the first time Zero had ever shown any
kind of attraction to her. Was it because she was sharing
a bed with him? *Crap.* Her thoughts were all over the
place and not making any sense at all.

Leaving the door, she went to the closet and
pulled out one of his shirts. All of her clothes were still at
home. She would need to stop by and collect some
things. There was no way she would be spending
however long it took for Alan to be caught wearing other
people's clothes.

She took out one of his shirts then headed into the
bathroom. After a quick shower she dried her body,

combed her hair, then used his toothbrush to clean her teeth. The bathroom door opened. Zero stood without a shirt.

Ink covered his body. Crossing her legs, she stared at her reflection and continued to brush her teeth. He wasn't sex on legs, and she didn't want anything to do with him. Zero was her brother's best friend, and they were friends. Nothing was going to happen. She tried to convince herself not to be attracted to him. Nothing was working.

"That's my shirt and my toothbrush."

"You didn't grab any of my stuff. I've got nothing here." She finished her teeth and gave him her full attention. He was climbing into the shower, showing his perfectly sculptured ass.

She wondered what it would be like to sink her nails into his flesh as he rode her hard. Maybe she should flick his butt with a towel to teach him a lesson. Prue decided against it. His ass was a delight, and she didn't want to ruin it by marking him.

"Fine, we'll go tomorrow. Stop checking out my ass."

Angered at how right he was about her checking out his ass, she flushed the toilet, smiling as he screamed at the sudden hit of cold water washing over him.

"Bitch, I'll get you for that," he said.

"Yeah, yeah." She wasn't afraid of Zero.

Settling into bed, she rolled to her side, punched the pillow and tried to get comfortable on the new bed. She heard Zero singing in the shower and grimaced. He was many things, but a singer wasn't one of them. She didn't see chart success in his future.

His scent surrounded her. The bed smelled like him. It was strong and had an answering pulse in her veins.

Wrapping the blanket around her, she got comfortable as Zero entered the room.

He flicked the lock on the door then climbed in behind her. She didn't argue. Rolling over, she lifted her leg and felt how very naked he actually he was. Jerking away, she glared at him. "Put some shorts on at least."

"This is my bed. I sleep naked in it. Get used to it." He smiled sweetly at her.

"You're being an asshole," she said.

"No, I'm being comfortable."

Smiling back at him, she leaned over his chest to turn the lamp off that he must have put on. "Be careful in the morning. I don't always see well. My glasses are in the bathroom, and I can crush a ball if I'm not careful." She flicked the light off, settling back into bed.

His heat made it hard for her to relax again.

Zero was naked, sleeping beside her. He wasn't asleep yet.

"He's out there somewhere," she said, thoughts returning to Alan. "He's thinking of ways of hurting us."

"Me. Alan wants to hurt me, no one else." His arm moved across her stomach. He dragged her close, and he settled his nose against her neck. "You smell good."

"Don't do that," she said. But Prue didn't pull away.

She felt the length of his cock against her ass. Sandy was right. He was rock hard. Rolling her eyes, she settled on her pillow listening to him breathing.

"We'll take care of everything, Prue. There's nothing we can do until he wants us to know." He kissed her neck, sighing. "I'm pleased to have you back."

"I can feel it."

"We'll talk about it some other time. Let me hold you for now and have this with you."

She wanted to argue but saw no use in it. Her body was alight with need for him.

Zero was unlike all of the men she'd been with before.

"I wish Trevor was with us."

"Right now, I don't." He kissed her neck.

Prue smiled at his response. She felt alive from his kisses alone.

****

Butch walked out of the clubhouse, opening and closing the small gate. He needed to see Cheryl one last time. After tonight he wasn't going to risk seeing her with the danger of Alan watching. The last couple of days he hadn't been able to stop thinking about her. Her face would find its way into his thoughts, and then a need to be with her would consume him.

Walking down the street, he took his time getting into town. He made his way toward the back heading to the church. The door was open again, and he took a seat. Cheryl was nowhere to be seen. Sitting down, he watched the front of the church wanting to see her.

After twenty minutes, he knew she wasn't there and left making his way to her house. She didn't live with her mother. The house was small and had homes on either side of her. He couldn't imagine living in such a small home.

Not all people have the luxury The Skulls offer you.

Knocking on the door, he stepped back and waited. A light was switched on, and then Cheryl opened the door. The lock stopped her from opening the door wide. "Butch? What are you doing here?"

"I had to come and see you," he said.

She looked past him. "It's really late."

"Something is going down at the club." He

stopped himself from spilling everything. Why did he feel at ease telling her everything? Clenching his teeth together, he glanced down at the ground. "Look, I won't hurt you. I just need to see you."

"I don't know you."

"I won't hurt you." He stepped close to her, wishing he could touch her.

Back off, you'll scare her.

Cheryl stared at him for several minutes before she closed the door. He heard the lock being moved, and then the door opened again. "I don't know why I'm doing this." She moved out of the way letting him pass.

"I swear I won't hurt you."

Why was he here?"

She took him toward her small kitchen. He saw a table with two chairs on either side. "Is your son in bed?"

"Yeah, he's in bed."

He watched her move to the kettle, filling it with water from the tap before returning it back to start heating.

"I work at the church. It doesn't mean you can come here all the time," she said, rubbing her hands down her sides. Did he make her nervous? "I let you in because you're a Skull. I know you're not going to hurt me."

"I wouldn't hurt you. I wanted to see you. Where is your man?"

"I don't know. He wanted nothing to do with me when he knocked me up. It's just my son and me." She turned away to look at her counter. Cheryl took a cloth, wiping away some dirt. He stared at her back seeing how long her hair was. The length surrounded her.

"What are you doing working at the church?"

"I may be a single mother, but it doesn't mean I can't work at the bloody church." She placed his cup in front of him, taking a seat opposite.

"Whoa, I wasn't saying shit."

She glared at him. "I work at the church because it makes *me* feel good. I like it." Cheryl took a sip of her drink, looking down at the table.

"The father just upped and left you?"

"Yeah. He was all for the planting but not for the growing and anything else."

Butch frowned. "Have you just compared having a kid to a plant growing?"

"It's not much different."

"You're something else, Cheryl."

He caught the smile she was hiding by her cup. Yep, he was truly fucked.

Chapter Seven

One week into the lockdown and Alan wasn't anywhere in sight. Whizz was having no luck in finding out what happened to him immediately after the accident. Hacking into the hospital records close to the burn site brought the identity of Alan, or at least a John Doe with need for surgery to the face, back along with the burns. From the documents, Alan hadn't given away his identity, and they'd only caught onto the description of the damage from what Zero told Whizz. After one year in the hospital, John Doe was transported out of the country where he just disappeared off the map. There was no other record of his progress. From the looks of it, Alan had found someone to take care of his needs without having it documented.

It was easy to do providing the person had funds. Not all of Alan's funds were known. Whizz was going through different countries, but hacking into private systems took time. Not only was Whizz working on his identity and where he'd be, he was helping with protection, taking time away from the computer.

Alex was trying to work with Ned to find out all they could. They were looking for a man who disappeared ten years ago to never be seen again. There was only so much Whizz could get out of the computer. They were all pulling their weight in trying to find out the answers to the mystery. Zero heaved out the trash as he watched Prue look after the kids. It was lockdown, but Tiny was letting them all out to play. The gates were locked, and they were not having any customers on their mechanic side.

Wiping the sweat from his brow, he watched Prue push one of the kids in a swing. It looked like Darcy, Blaine's daughter. What would it be like having a kid with Prue? Their nights were spent not talking about the obvious attraction between them. More times than not she woke up to his rock hard cock digging in her ass. He knew she did as he was awake most of the time. She didn't knee his balls though.

"She's something special," Sophia said, standing beside him.

He glanced toward the woman he'd had a crush on for the good part of the year. Since Prue had entered his life again he hadn't give Sophia much of a thought. Fuck, he hadn't even noticed that he wasn't looking at the other woman. When the fuck did that happen?

He returned his attention to Prue. "Yeah, she really is."

"I hope there are no hard feelings." Sophia smiled up at him. "We would never have worked, and I imagine you know that."

"You're Nash's woman."

"No, it's not just because I'm Nash's woman." She looked at Prue then back at him. "You'll figure it out soon enough."

What was it with people around him telling him to figure shit out when it came to Prue?

When he heard her giggling and laughing, he turned to see what had caused her to be so happy. He saw her on the ground surrounded by kids. His heart filled with joy at the sight before him.

"See, she means more to you than you even realize." Sophia touched his arm, smiled at him, then moved away. He followed her movements, unsure what the feeling was clawing in his gut. Instead of following after Sophia, he made his way toward Prue as she called to him far more than Sophia. Tugging one of the little ones off, he spun the little guy around. Darcy was laughing as she tried to tickle Prue.

"Save me," Prue said, pressing a hand to her forehead. "They're attacking me. My prince, save me from these little people."

In no time at all Zero was laughing along with all the kids and Prue. Messing around, he ended up on the floor right alongside Prue. Only when Eva shouted "lunch" did the kids scamper off. Darcy wrapped her arms around her neck. "I really like you, Aunty Prue. Don't leave."

The little girl was gone, and Prue let out a sigh.

"I really like you as well. I don't want you to leave." He took hold of her hand, locking their fingers together. She tightened her grip around his palm. Zero wanted her to stay with him in Fort Wills.

"I like being here with you. My life is not here though. I've got a life away from all of this." They'd gone to her house the day after they shared a bed. He'd looked at her collection of pictures of the three of them together. It was her, him, and Trevor against the world after her parents died.

"I don't want you to go home."

"Zero," she said, about to move.

He held her hand tighter, stopping her from leaving his side.

"No, listen to me. I don't want you to go. This has nothing to do with Alan. He's a problem, but him being here has made me realize how much I miss you. I miss this." He pointed his hand up at the sky. The clouds were drifting by in the blue sky.

"That one looks like a duck," she said, pointing straight up.

"I thought it looked like a man with a big cock." He titled his head to the side.

"Everything to you has a big cock. You've not changed at all, have you?"

Zero held her hand tighter. They pointed at clouds saying what they thought they were. Prue's ideas were tame enough to be heard by children. His would need an adult censor.

"You've got a dirty mind," she said, sitting up. "You're always changing the conversation."

He didn't let go of her hand and got to his feet. Zero led her over to the swings.

"Do you have any idea how big my ass is?" she asked, looking at the seat then over at him.

"Stop being a pain in my ass. That's Tate's job. Sit down."

She rolled her eyes and took a seat. Moving behind her, he placed his hand on her back. Zero didn't push her. Placing his hand on her back, he stayed close. "I'm not going to give up on this," he said.

"On what?"

"On you staying in Fort Wills."

"There's nothing here for me."

Giving her a gentle push, he watched her start to move. Using both palms, he applied pressure each time she swung back to him. Her hands held the metal chain tightly.

"There's me. I'm here for you."

"You'd scare away all potential dates. I would never get some light relief for my needs."

Teeth clenched, he slowly brought her to a stop. He stepped in front of her, sinking his fingers into her hair. "Why are you trying to test me?"

"I'm not trying. I'm succeeding." She smiled and stuck her tongue out.

Breaking the distance between them, Zero slammed his lips on top of hers. He heard her gasp seconds before he slid his tongue into her mouth. With his free hand, he cupped her cheek, stroking the tips of his fingers down to caress her neck. Her pulse pounded against his fingers.

Zero didn't want to let go.

Deepening the kiss, he watched her close her eyes and tilt her head to the side. Fisting his hand in her hair, he tugged on the length hearing her moan. She liked the bite of pain, did she? He could work with that.

Her legs were open, and he slid between them. He moved his fingers from her neck down to stroke her breast. Her nipple was rock hard to the touch.

Pulling away, he waited for her to open her eyes. They were smoky, lust filled green eyes staring back at him. Was she as fiery as her red hair? Zero had a feeling she would rival any flame between the sheets.

Prue would be a true gem to possess and own.

"We could have this together," he said, sliding his fingers down her stomach to reach the waistband of her jeans. Her breath heaved with each indrawn breath she took.

Releasing her hair, he stroked a finger over her bottom lip.

"You've got a thing for Sophia. I will not be some piece of ass you use to satisfy your need for her."

"This is not about Sophia," he said.

"Yeah?"

He nodded.

"I've heard them talk, Zero. You've had a crush on her, thought yourself in love with her, for the better part of a year." He listened to every word she spoke, detecting the pain she felt. "We've been together for over two weeks, nearing three. How can you fall out of love with someone that fast?"

"I'm not in love with Sophia."

"The shiner Nash gave you is proof to me you overstepped the line. I'm not as dumb as you think I am.

Every time we were together and you talked about this club, I listened." She pushed some hair out of her eyes. He held the chains, refusing to back away. "You talked about Sophia, especially in drink. You said her beauty would never be rivaled."

"I was drunk."

"And yet it was how you felt. I'm not stupid, Zero."

"I don't want you to go. There is something between us."

She placed her hand on his chest and pushed. He took a step back and another as she got to her feet. "We may have attraction, but I will not be the second choice because the woman you really want is not available to you. I care about you."

"What do I have to do to show you?" he asked.

"Prove to me she doesn't affect you anymore."

"How the fuck do I do that?"

He watched as she made to walk away.

"I don't know. I guess I'll know when I see it." She spun away and headed back to the clubhouse.

"Fuck," he said, shouting the word aloud. Butch walked up to him, smiling.

"I take it your woman doesn't accept any of your shit." Butch lit a cigarette, sitting down on one of the swings.

"What are you doing out here?" he asked.

"They're attempting to feed a pack of animals. I tell you, there is nothing scarier than seeing a bunch of kids hungry." Butch shivered as he stared somewhere past Zero's shoulder. "What's up with Prue?"

"She doesn't want to fuck me because she thinks I've got a thing for Sophia."

"You *have* got a thing for Sophia," Butch said, frowning at him. "Fuck, the whole club knows you've got a thing for that woman. The only one who didn't know was Sophia, and Nash soon put her in the know. She's been avoiding you for some time."

Couldn't have been avoiding him that much. She was fucking talking to him earlier.

"It's not what you think. I'm not in love with her." Zero didn't know what to say to make Prue realize he was telling the truth. Something had struck him hard being around Prue for so long. Was that it? Being around Prue made him understand his feelings for another?

Crap, he didn't understand what the fuck was going on.

"What's up your ass?" Zero asked, changing the subject.

"Nothing. I'm more than happy with life."

Whatever, asshole.

Zero was jealous at the happiness in his friend's face. He would be happy when Prue finally gave him a chance.

****

Prue helped with the dishes while cursing Zero and his stupid, weak attempt to seduce her. She had been approached in the playground by nine year olds with more charisma than he just displayed. Picking up the last plate, she dried it viciously before putting it on the pile of others.

"Stupid, fucking asshole," she said, muttering the words underneath her breath.

"Whoa, who has you pissed off?" Tate asked, walking into the room. She carried a glass of water.

"Nothing." Prue wasn't in the mood for whatever this bitch had to throw at her.

"I'm calling a truce," Tate said, holding her hands out in front of her.

"What?"

"I can't get Murphy to tell me what's going on. My dad refuses, and Eva is following his lead. Everyone stops talking when I enter a room. It irritates me. I don't like it."

"I'm not going to tell you anything," Prue said, pointing at her chest. "I'm new here. Tiny looks like a scary guy. I'm not going to do anything to piss him off. If you want the truth then you're going to have to get it out of them."

"I understand." Tate ran fingers through her hair. "Look, I'm a bitch. I know I'm a bitch. You're Zero's woman, and I don't want to cause problems. We're all on lockdown. It takes a toll, and I don't want to be fighting with the new girl, especially seeing as you've got the others on your side as well."

"This is what this is about?"

"No, I want us to be friends. This club means everything to my family. I fuck up all the time, but they've always got my back."

Prue thought about it. She didn't know how long Alan intended to play whatever game he wanted to play. "Fine, we can be friends."

She offered her hand, and Tate took it.

Seconds later Tate left the room, and Prue left the kitchen, going to Zero's room. She was surprised to see him on his bed. "I thought you were outside."

"Eva's got the kids settled in front of a movie. I don't know how long it's going to last, and I wanted to spend some time with you."

Taking a seat beside him, she gazed down at the floor. Club life was not what she expected. "I'm surprised you can stay here for so long. When we were younger you always needed to do things, to get out there and live your life."

"It hasn't changed. The families are here, and so

everything is toned down. None of the sweet-butts are naked waiting for a fuck. The alcohol is being limited to after eight at night. Lockdown means a lockdown on everything, pussy, booze, fun."

"Nah, I don't believe that." She took his hand, leading him downstairs to the room with the pool table. Staying in the bedroom alone with Zero was not going to be good for her sticking to her rules. He was too much of a temptation to be alone with a bed and plenty of time on their hands. Once they were surrounded by other club members she was safe. "There is more to life than booze and pussy. We can have fun without getting drunk." She handed him a pool stick. "Let's just play and try to forget why we're here. You know, like other people have fun. It's not some foreign concept, Zero."

He took the stick from her looking at the pool table. "How long has it been since you played?"

Trevor had taught her how to play pool. She pressed the button releasing the balls and started to arrange them within the plastic triangle. "It has been too long. I'm going to shoot first to check my aim."

She felt his gaze on her as she aligned her stick and started hitting the balls. Once they were spread out she took her time shooting them all into the holes available. A couple of the men were watching them. Zero was smiling in the corner as she potted the last ball. Prue hadn't done them in any order. Playing pool had been something she did with Trevor and Zero to pass the time when they were younger.

"You were just showing off," Zero said, moving away from the wall.

"Was not. I've not played pool since before Trevor died." She turned away so he wouldn't witness her pain at remembering her brother.

He grabbed her shoulder, pulling her close to

press a kiss to her neck. "I miss him, too, baby. You don't need to hide your feelings from me. I know what you're feeling. Come on, let's play."

Prue arranged the balls but let Zero take his shot. For the next hour they played pool, listening to the men take bets on each of them. She was surprised how many men betted on her winning.

When it came to the last shot, Prue was crowned the winner. She chuckled as Zero bowed down to her.

Eva shouted that dinner was ready. Leaving the pool room, she was making her way out of the room when Zero snagged her arm tugging her against him. The wall was to her back, and he crowded around her stopping her from going anywhere.

"What do you think you're doing?" she asked, looking up into his eyes. They were in dangerous territory, very dangerous territory, and alarm bells were going off inside her head.

"Why haven't you played pool in a long time?"

"Seriously? This is why you're stopping me from getting fed." She made to brush past him. Zero wouldn't let her leave using his body to trap her against the wall.

"I know you, Prue. You love playing pool. Why haven't you kept on playing it?"

"Is this really important to you?"

"Trevor and I spent weeks teaching you after you nagged us. We could have been doing anything, and instead we trained your ass to shoot and now you're telling me you haven't even put it into practice?" His palm slammed the wall beside her head. She wasn't afraid, but the heat filling her panties was another problem altogether.

Don't fall for him. It would be a big mistake. A big fucking mistake.

He's in love with Sophia.

Take him, fuck him, and get it out of your system.

"Pool is something you, Trevor, and I played. When he died and you were not around, I didn't want to share it with anyone else. It was our thing. No one else could ever compete. He was my brother, and you're my friend. Can't you believe for one minute that I missed you?" she asked.

"What? Prue, I came around."

"You came around when it suited you. You called me when it suited you. I had nothing to do with it." She stopped, looking past his shoulder. "In the early days after Trevor died you visited me regularly, but then they eventually turned into once a year. Shooting pool, messing around, drinking, shooting, it always reminds me of the time all three of us spent together, and it hurts. It hurts so bad that at times I can't even breathe."

"Nothing is ever going to bring him back."

"I know this." She stamped her foot in anger. "I know I can never have him back. There is no magic wand to turn the clock back. I know the reality, Zero. It's fucking hard, and it hurts like hell. So no, I don't play pool. I don't do anything other than study and mark papers. I cannot let myself remember because it hurts."

His arms wrapped around her, and it was only then that Prue realized tears were pouring out of her eyes. She was hurting, and the pain wouldn't stop. Trevor was gone. Zero was in love with someone else, and she was all alone.

"I've got you, Prue. Let it all go."

She held onto him tightly as she released ten years of pain and anguish. When Trevor first died, she was sad and she cried for days. There came a point when she could no longer cry as life demanded she still take part. Bills always needed to be paid, and life had to go on without her brother. She stopped crying, pushing all the pain and heartache to one side.

Being around Zero opened her up to wounds she truly believed had healed.

"They're going to think I'm a right girl." She sobbed the words against his chest.

"No, they're not. You're a woman who has been shot and seen shit you should never have seen. You need this, and while you're crying I need to hold you." He kissed the top of her head. Releasing a breath she glanced up at him. "I could have lost you, Prue. I failed Trevor. I cannot, will not fail you."

"You don't owe me anything."

"It's not about a debt needing to be repaid. I care about you, Prue. The thought of anything happening to you makes me feel sick. It's not happening. Alan can go and rot. I will spend the rest of my days on lockdown if it means I can guarantee your safety."

She smiled. It was a sweet thought, but even she couldn't handle a lifetime of being stuck in the same place.

Wiping her eyes, she felt her old self again. She was emotionally drained. Her stomach growled, letting her need for food be heard.

"I better feed you before you faint on me." His arms stayed around her shoulders holding her close. They entered the main clubhouse. All the tables had been put together for all the people to sit around. Two chairs were left free between Eva and Murphy.

"Is everything all right?" Tiny asked.

She nodded.

"Yeah, everything's good," Zero said, reaching for the chicken.

Prue filled her plate with roast chicken, salad, and potatoes. She didn't have the appetite to eat but knew she needed something to keep her going. The conversation went over her head. Her thoughts were elsewhere, and she didn't have the energy to keep up.

****

"Why don't you just blow the clubhouse up?"

Alan thought about the question coming Peter. The men were not well known for their education. They were still loyal men even if they were a bit on the stupid side. The Skulls were on lockdown, but that didn't mean they were kept inside the one building. The children were still walking around the compound.

Looking at the new photos he'd been given, Alan smiled. The compound was on lockdown. No one could get in, but it didn't stop them from coming out. Gates and fences wouldn't keep everything out. He had his own way of getting what he wanted.

"Blow the clubhouse up. Where is the fun in that?" Alan asked, glancing up at Peter.

"It kills the people you want, deals with The Skulls, and we can be gone." Peter shrugged.

"This is not about moving on and getting the job done quickly. Something like this needs to take time, precision, and patience. It's a game I've learned to play for a long time." Alan pinned the pictures up one by one. The best way to get the mouse was by setting little traps. Zero was getting comfortable. The cheese was in reach. Soon it would be his time to strike.

"This is far more dangerous. The Skulls is not a club to be messed with," Peter said.

Alan had heard all about The Lions, the drug dealers, and even The Darkness, trying to pick off The Skulls. "I'm not after the club. I don't want Fort Wills. The only thing I want is to watch this man suffer. I'm going to tear his world apart and laugh while I do it." He pointed to the picture of Zero. The man in the photo looked so happy. By the time Alan was finished, Zero wouldn't have the first clue how to smile, and then he'd be dead. "Don't worry, my friends. Everything will be happening all in good time."

Ten years he'd waited. Ten years of surviving, learning to walk once again and then losing the one he loved had taught him a great deal. Revenge would be his when the time was right.

Patience was a virtue. One he'd learned to embrace.

Chapter Eight

The following Friday, Alan still hadn't made his move. Prue was much recovered, and her wound was nothing more than a scar, a vicious memory she would take with her when it was all over. The painkillers she'd been taking were no longer necessary. Glancing out of the window of his bedroom Zero saw night had fallen. After dinner he listened to the women put the kids to bed, getting them out of the way so the alcohol could be fast flowing. The sweet-butts were allowed to mingle with the single men, keeping their clothes on until they were alone in a bedroom. Tiny kept to the rules during lockdown. No one was allowed to break them either. Zero had no reason to break the rules. Prue was already in his bed.

He watched the door to the bathroom open, and Prue stood before him in a plain black dress that showed off her large cleavage and clung to her curves. She looked fucking stunning. His cock swelled at the sight of her.

She'd twisted her red hair up on top of her head, exposing the length of her neck. The desire to run kisses all over her neck was strong. He resisted and watched as she bent forward to put on a pair of heels.

Fucking hell, he was not going to survive the night. In the past Zero had watched her dress up to go on dates. She'd been a tomboy, and wearing a denim skirt down to her ankles had been the closest she got to feminine. The woman before him didn't have a single inch of tomboy about her. She was temptation, sex, and lust all rolled into one.

"Do you want to close your mouth? It looks like you're drooling, and it's not such a good look for you." She chuckled, smoothing her palms over her legs. "How do I look?"

"We're not going out. It's only the club members here," he said, hoping none of the men would try to hit on her. There was only so much he could handle, and pushing away all of his friends because they wanted her didn't feel like much fun. He had better ways of spending his night. One of them was with his hand wrapped around his cock rather than watching Prue in that dress.

"I want to dress up and be pretty for once. Stop ruining my buzz, or I swear I will kick you in the balls so you can never father children." She raised a brow at him.

Laughing, he walked right up to her. Cupping her cheek, he stared into her beautiful green eyes knowing he was lost. She truly was a beauty.

"There is a lot more I can think of that you can do to my balls."

Her cheeks grew red. She didn't drop her gaze. This is what he loved about her. Prue never backed down from a fight.

"I'm sure you can." She pressed a hand to his chest. "Just like I can think of a few things you can do with that mouth of yours." Prue went on her toes, kissing his lips. "Tonight is about fun. Alan has not popped out of the woodwork. We've got a small window of having fun."

Alan's name sucked all the arousal out of his body. Whizz couldn't find anything yet. The trail ended about five years ago, which sucked. At the moment, Zero didn't care. With the threat of Alan, he still had Prue in his bed. Once the other man was gone, he'd have to fight to keep her with him in Fort Wills. No one knew what Alan looked like seeing as Zero fucked his face up ten years ago. The sketch provided didn't help either. The hospital room had been dark, and Prue could only remember so much with all the stress and pain.

"Come on." He took her hand leading her downstairs. Music was playing from the stereo in the corner. Steven was playing barman while the others were sitting around talking, smoking, drinking, or playing cards. "Are you up for a game of pool?" he asked.

"Not yet. We played not long ago." She wrinkled her nose going straight for the bar. Zero couldn't take his gaze off her.

Prue's body looked so inviting.

Sitting at the bar, he listened to her order a beer. Steven handed him a beer, which he thanked the man for.

"How are you finding club life?" Steven asked, staring at Prue's tits.

Taking a large gulp of his beer, he wondered what he was supposed to do with the man looking at his woman's tits.

Not your woman. She won't let you claim her.

"It's a little boring. I bet when the lockdown is lifted and Alan is gone, it will be fun." Prue tilted the bottle to her lips.

He watched her throat swallow the liquid. There shouldn't be anything erotic in the sight. His cock was saying otherwise. Her lips would look so fucking beautiful wrapped around his dick. Zero would love to see her throat swallow his cum.

"Give me a whiskey," he said, trying to get rid of Steven.

Seconds later a glass of whiskey was placed in front of him.

"You sure look pretty," Steven said.

"Fuck off." Zero growled the words at the other man. He was sick and tired of Steven trying to get on her good side.

"Zero! That was rude," she said.

He glared down at her. She shoved him hard in

the shoulder before storming away. Watching her disappear he rounded on Steven, who had his arms in the air. "Hey, man, cool it. I'm not in the mood to lose a limb. She's taken, I get it."

"Yeah, she is taken."

Butch chose that moment to plonk down on the bar stool. "Actually, you kind of need to claim her before you do that."

"You're supposed to be my friend," Zero said, turning his attention to the other man.

"I am your friend. You can't go warning off brothers without intending to take her off the market."

"What about your own woman?" Zero asked, recalling Butch's confession the other day.

"She's still on the market and has nothing to do with the club." Butch leaned in close. "Shit is going to hit the fan sooner or later. Alan is not going away. I'd take the time while you have the chance to claim her. Once Alan starts, he's never going to stop." Zero's glass was swiped out of his hand. "Think about it."

Leaning against the bar he saw Prue playing cards with Rose and Hardy. It wouldn't be long before Rose was naked and Hardy was showing her off to the rest of the club.

Prue's tits caught Zero's attention. Sipping his whiskey, he watched her lean forward to grab a card. She wasn't like other women. Prue didn't give a fuck about her nails or going shopping for clothes. Not once had she talked about breaking a nail. She got stuck in with the kids and with the work.

The other day he'd even seen her fixing a bike up with Blaine.

She really was a one of a kind woman.

When she grew bored with losing cards, she grabbed a bottle of vodka from the shelf, leaving some money for Steven.

"Come on then," she said, taking his hand.

"What?"

"Let's go and play pool. I'd rather play something I've got a chance of winning rather than not."

Zero followed her into the pool room. Killer and Kelsey were playing, and they joined them for a game. They teamed up and played the other two. Standing behind Prue, Zero stared at her ass. The dress she wore rode up her back, exposing the top part of her legs.

Killer constantly whispered in Kelsey's ear. The other woman was giggling and turning red at whatever the other man was saying. One of the shots required Prue to lean over the table.

Staying behind her, he watched as she aligned the shot and got the perfect view of her red covered pussy. Fuck, she was wearing red panties. Zero failed every shot after he saw her sweet pussy.

Prue took over, annoyed, and beat Killer and Kelsey five games to one. Prue giggled, kissing Killer's cheek as they left the room.

Banding an arm around her waist, he knew she was getting merry from the drink.

Rose was up on the table with Hardy behind her. Prue paused as they stopped and stared at the woman erotically dancing around the pole at the furthest end of the room.

"So that's why there is a pole there," she said, gasping.

"Hardy and Rose are known for showing off in front of everyone. They will do everything in front of an audience. His one rule is not to touch. Rose is his woman. If they touch, he'll hurt them."

She moaned, wriggling her ass against his cock.

He gripped her hips, hissing. "Be careful, baby.

I'm holding on by a thread."

"Are you wanting to fuck me, Zero?" she said, glancing over her shoulder up at him.

"You know I do."

Prue turned around, sliding a finger down his chest until she cupped his cock. "I'm wet, Zero."

Spinning her so her back was pressed to the wall, Zero gazed down into her eyes. "Do you have any idea what you're doing?" he asked.

"I'm not drunk. I'm happy. I'm relaxed, and I can't think of a single reason why we can't fuck. It has been weeks, Zero, months." She leaned in close, pressing kisses to his neck. He groaned as she bit down on the flesh of his neck. "It has been so long since I've felt a nice hard cock pounding inside me."

"You don't know what you're doing," he said.

He couldn't get any more turned on. His cock was so fucking tight. Zero imagined the imprint of his zipper would be on his cock.

She grabbed his hand, bringing his fingers to her mouth. He watched her open her mouth and suck one then two fingers into her mouth, getting them nice and wet.

"What's the matter, Zero? You never have a woman tell you what she wants?" she asked.

Zero didn't respond as she moved his fingers up the inside her of her thigh. He cupped her heat, feeling the wetness of her panties against his palm.

No, he couldn't wait anymore. Grabbing her hand, it was his turn to lead, and he took her upstairs to his room.

****

Prue was melting, and the alcohol she'd consumed had given her the courage to finally approach Zero with her need. Sleeping next to him every night and not being with him was driving her crazy. Most of her dreams were filled with sex and wanton need. There was only so much she could survive. Refusing Zero was no longer an option.

When Alan finally lashed out she needed to keep her wits about her. The only way to deal with that was to give in to their need.

Zero opened his bedroom door. She turned in time to see him flick the lock into place. He was breathing deeply. "Wow, you move fast, don't you?" she said, smiling.

Her panties were soaked with her need.

Reaching behind her, she pulled the pins out of her hair, letting the length fall around her shoulders. His gaze hadn't left hers. Zero also hadn't spoken a word to her since he got her to his room.

"What's the matter? Cat got your tongue?"

"Take the dress off. Keep the shoes on."

Raising a brow, she placed her hands on her hips. "You're going to order me about?"

"And you're going to do as you're told. We're not best friends right now, Prue. This is my room, and you've got no control here. I get what I want."

He turned her on, standing up to her.

"Okay." She wasn't going to argue. He could be the boss all he wanted. She was more than happy to give him the reins in the bedroom.

She tugged at the hem of her dress and dragged it up her legs before pulling it over her head. Throwing the dress at him, she stood in the modest black heels and a matching set of red lace underwear. The bra felt good against her skin while the panties made her feel sensual.

"Fuck me," he said.

Staying still, she waited for his next instruction.

Zero threw the dress aside before removing his

jacket. When his shirt came off, her mouth dried up at the sight. She'd seen him without a shirt plenty of times. This was different. They were going to fuck, and their friendship was going to change. The line had been drawn years ago. Between the two of them, they were smashing down all barriers that kept them apart.

He took a step closer wearing his jeans and boots.

Staring up at him, they stood close but not touching. The masculine scent of his deodorant wafted up to her nostrils. Licking her lips, she gazed at the expanse of his chest.

"You've got me here. Tell me what you want."

His hands reached out, gripping some of her hair and cupping her face. Zero tilted her head back, leaning in close. "I want a kiss."

Zero took possession of her mouth, sliding his tongue inside. She whimpered at the power he held over her from a simple kiss. Plenty of men had kissed her before. None of them had left her yearning so much. His tongue teased hers, deepening the kiss.

Gripping his arms, she held onto his body as she went a little lightheaded. He didn't move or try to touch another part of her.

His lips and hands were the only parts of him touching her. She sank her nails into his arms, wanting him to take control, bend her over the bed and fuck her.

"Please," she said. Zero kissed down her neck, sucking on the pulse at the side.

"Why are you in such a rush to have it over with?" he asked.

"I'm not. Please, fuck me." She wasn't above begging. The heat built in her pussy, and she was on fire.

"I will. All in good time. My room, my rules, and you're going to do everything I tell you." He bit her skin, making her gasp with pleasure before he returned to her lips.

"This is not fair."

"By the time I'm finished you're going to know what being fucked by me is all about. I don't do sloppy. When I fuck, it's wet, dirty, and fucking memorable. I don't waste my time." He tugged on her hair forcing her to take a step back.

Zero kept this up until she once again had her back to the wall. He pressed his body to hers, grinding his rock hard cock against her stomach. "You want a quick fuck that leaves you wanting more then find someone else. I will have you screaming for me to stop from what I do to you."

Prue whimpered. "I want you."

"Then you do not order me around. You do as I tell you and accept what I do to you." He fisted her hair in his hand, tugging until she was staring at the ceiling. His lips moved around her neck going from ear to ear before moving down to suck on her nipple through the lace of her bra.

She screamed at the pleasure. He bit down on the hard bud adding some pain to the heat of his mouth. Zero went to the next nipple, sucking the bud into his mouth before biting down. The pleasure and pain mixed together leaving her jerking in his arms.

"I can smell your pussy, baby. I've not even got my hands on you, and you're fucking hot to the touch." He knelt before her. His hands still held her head back, forcing her to look at the ceiling. She felt his face press against her pussy. His tongue flicked across the lace, keeping him away from her clit.

"Please," she said, screaming.

"Do you want me or a man who doesn't know his dick from his elbow?" he asked, growling the words against the flesh of her thigh.

"You, I want you." Fuck, he was more than she ever imagined, and all he'd done was touch her with his lips. He released her hair enough for her to look at him. Zero stood up, staring down into her eyes. He was so much taller than she was.

"Good choice," he said.

His hands released her. In quick movements he turned her to face the wall, flicking the catch of her bra. He tugged the straps down her arms, throwing the red lace onto the floor. Next, he rid her body of the panties, getting her to step out of them.

She watched him place a chair beside her.

"Put your foot on the chair."

Frowning, she did as he asked. His fingers started at the curve of her ankle and slowly worked his fingers up the inside her thigh.

"Your body is to die for," he said, caressing her thigh, gently. "Your skin is soft, but your legs are strong."

Biting her lip, she gasped as he cupped her naked pussy.

"You're soaking wet. Do you want me to leave you, or should I slide my finger through this slit to see how fucking wet you are?" he asked.

"Please," she said, moaning for more. "Touch me. Don't stop."

"Oh, I will touch you. I'll have you begging for me."

One finger glided through the lips of her sex. Panting for breath, she screamed out at the sudden touch to her clit.

"Yes, that's right, baby. You're so fucking wet and beautiful." He tapped her clit several times. Down his finger went to slide into her cunt. "Now there is perfection. Tight, wet, and ready to take a cock. You want my cock, baby?"

"Yes." Her body no longer felt like her own.

Zero owned her.

A second finger was added to the first, stretching her pussy. "Fuck, you're going to make it hard for me to fuck you."

He pumped two fingers inside her, adding a third when she grew wetter.

"I'm not going to do anything else until I hear you cry out. I want your cum all over my fingers, Prue."

She whimpered. Holding her leg up on the chair was hard to do as he worked her pussy. His other hand held onto her hips, keeping her in place.

"Are you going to give me what I want? Or do I have to take it?" he asked.

Shaking her head, Prue closed her eyes concentrating on his fingers. They were hard and rough from the labor he did every day. He moved his three fingers up, gliding over her clit. "I can feel how close you are." Zero thrust the three fingers inside her cunt. "Are you on birth control?"

"I get the shot. I don't know if the painkiller affected it or not."

"Then I'll wear a condom. Soon, I'll take you without a condom. I want to see my cum filling you up."

He was a lot dirtier than she imagined. For some reason she'd always thought Zero would be a little more reserved in the bedroom.

"Do I surprise you?" he asked.

"A little." She moaned as his thumb pressed to her clit.

"Why?"

"I didn't think you would be like this."

Zero claimed her lips in response. He bit into her bottom lip.

"Baby, I like my sex a lot dirtier than this," he said, whispering against her ear. "The things I want to do to you are not fit for tender ears. Do you think you can handle it?"

Her orgasm crashed through her. Zero held her up with an arm wrapped around her waist. He didn't let up, stroking her clit throughout her orgasm. His fingers left her pussy, leaving her feeling empty.

"Fuck yes," she said. "I can handle everything you throw at me."

Chapter Nine

Zero's fingers were soaked in her cream. Pulling them away from her body, he waited until she was looking at him before he licked her cum off, loving the taste of her sweet release. "I look forward to eating out your pussy. You're going to give me everything, aren't you, Prue?"

She nodded. Bless her, she looked so tired. The night was only just beginning. He wasn't going to give her a chance to regret what they were about to do. Lifting her up in his arms, he dumped her on the bed. She still wore those heels, and he wasn't about to remove them.

"Unbutton my jeans," he said, standing at the edge of the bed. The jeans needed to come off. They were strangling his rock hard cock. Her hands were shaking, and it took her multiple attempts to get the button open.

He didn't interfere and waited for her to get them open. Zero hissed when she slid the zipper across his erection. He was fucking hurting, he was so hard.

"Sorry," she said, mumbling the words.

"Take my cock out."

She pushed the jeans down his thighs, and his cock sprang free. Releasing a breath, he was so thankful to have the constraints off his cock. It had been a nightmare concentrating on fingering Prue's slick cunt while his cock was begging to slam inside her.

"Wow," she said.

Looking down at her head, he saw her gaze was on his dick. He'd been blessed with a good size cock. Zero worked well with what he had, and all the women he was with left him screaming his name. Gripping the base, he worked the length to the tip seeing the pre-cum leak out of the slit. "Lick it."

Prue didn't play bashful. Her hands went to his legs as she licked the cream coated tip. Her tongue was warm, making him gasp as she slid it across his length. She moaned, taking the whole of the tip.

Reaching out, he gripped her hair and pulled. She released his cock, staring up at him.

"What?" she asked.

"I didn't tell you to suck my cock, baby."

"I want to."

He smiled. "We don't always get what we want." Dropping his lips to hers, he kissed her to silence any protests. Stepping back, he kicked off his boots then removed the jeans, kicking them aside. Standing in front of her, he stared down the curves of her body. She had a lovely rounded stomach and full ass. "Go to your knees."

She didn't argue and went to her knees. He saw the puckered hole of her ass begging him to feel it.

"You ever been fucked in the ass?" he asked.

Prue looked at him over her shoulder. "Why do you want to know?"

"It doesn't matter if you have or not. I'm going to claim it either way." He stroked across her cheek, moaning at the scent coming off her. The smell of a cum-soaked pussy was the best smell in the world, at least to him it was.

"Yes," she said.

"When?"

"Over a year ago. I was with someone, and we did *a lot* together."

"Define a lot?" he asked, sliding a finger into her cunt. He watched his digits disappear knowing his cock was going to be sliding into her pussy very soon.

"We fucked in front of people. He liked for people to watch us together."

"Really?"

"Yes. He fucked my ass as well. We were not well suited for each other unless we were in the bedroom. He was my guy at the bar." She chuckled.

Zero nodded, not wanting to know anymore. Whoever the bastard was, he wouldn't be getting Prue again. Tonight was not going to be the only time they were together. Zero wasn't going to let her get away from him. Sliding his fingers into her heat, he heard her whimper. Sinking down to his knees, he caught her hips and pulled her close. Sliding his tongue into her pussy, he dropped down to tease her clit.

Her cum exploded on his tongue, and he swallowed it down, licking and sucking her. He pressed two fingers inside her pussy watching her take him.

When he could stand it no longer, he turned her around, drawing her to the edge of the bed to flick her clit with his tongue.

"Please, Zero, fuck me," she said, crying out.

Slapping her pussy, he saw her jerk then cover her face as she screamed. "When I'm good and ready. I want to taste your cum on my tongue."

Opening the lips of her sex, he stared down at her swollen clit. Her flesh was already wet from her previous orgasm. His cock was begging for some attention. Zero wasn't going to be selfish. Prue was going to get every minute of torture she'd given him for the past couple of weeks.

Every morning he woke up to her curvy ass pressed against his cock. She wriggled and stretched, making him want to fuck her.

Her presence alone was a constant distraction to him.

Zero tongued her clit, then slid down to plunge into her pussy. He lapped at her juices, keeping her open for what he wanted to do to her.

"Please," she said, begging.

Flicking her clit, he slid a finger inside her pussy. He turned his finger and stroked over her g-spot. Within seconds she splintered apart, hurtling into orgasm. Zero swallowed down her cum, and with the rest he coated her cunt getting her nice and slick.

When he was finished, he pushed her up the bed, crawling between her thighs. Her tits shook with each indrawn breath.

The condom.

Cursing, he left her side, grabbed a handful of condoms, and he threw them within reach. Tearing into the foil, he covered his cock with the latex protecting them both from the risk of pregnancy.

Neither of them spoke as he coated the latex with her cream. She was red and swollen from his touch.

Bumping her clit, he watched her trying to get away from his touch. Laughing, he held her hips, staring down into her eyes. "Are you not used to having multiple orgasms, baby?" he asked.

She shook her head.

"Not even with your adventurous lover?" he asked. "Didn't he make you come more than once?"

"No, he didn't."

Zero marked it against the other man and added a tick to his name. Gripping the base of his shaft, he eased his cock down to the entrance of her pussy. When the tip was inside, he returned his hand to her hips. Slowly, he pressed inside her cunt feeling the inner walls ripple with each inch he slid inside.

"Fuck, you're tight. Come on, baby, give me your tight little pussy."

Her gaze was on him, and Zero wanted her addicted to his touch. He tightened his hold on his hips, and with one thrust he embedded her on his cock. She screamed as he hit her cervix, going as deep as he could inside her.

"That's it, Prue. Take my cock."

She reached out, gripping the wooden slats of his headboard.

"Fuck, Zero," she said, screaming his name.

Looking down at her body, he leaned down sucking her nipple into his mouth.

"I told you I'd have you screaming my name." He waited for her to get accustomed to his length inside her. Zero sucked her nipple into his mouth then moved onto the next nipple, flicking the hard bud with his tongue.

Her cunt pulsed around his cock. Gritting his teeth, he bit down onto her nipple. Prue arched her back, pressing her chest toward him.

"You're doing this on purpose," she said.

"What am I doing on purpose?" he asked.

"You're torturing me for making you wait."

He smiled, kissing the side of her breast. "Maybe next time you'll learn your lesson and not make me wait." Sliding out of her tight warmth until only the tip remained inside her, Zero slammed in deep going to her cervix. For the next three thrusts he didn't give her a chance to get used to his invasion. He fucked her hard, taking what he wanted. The need to take her pussy and pound her until she forgot everything else was strong. Zero held himself back. He wanted her to want him, not be afraid to fuck him again.

She kept hold of the headboard as he fucked her. Her grip stopped her from hitting her head on the wall. Zero plundered her warmth, wishing more than anything that he didn't wear a condom. He wanted to feel her wet heat surround his naked shaft.

You want to put a baby inside her.

Gritting his teeth, he held onto her hips, tightly,

slamming in deep. The only sounds in the room were from their heavy breathing and moans. He released one hip to stroke her clit. She shook her head. "No, I can't."

"Yes, you can. You will give me your orgasm, or I will not let you come again."

She whimpered. Her eyes focused on him. They were glazed with lust and burning bright with her need.

"Give me what I want, Prue," he said.

Her clit was soaking from her release. His fingers glided through her slit with ease. Holding himself inside her, he stroked her clit.

Each caress had her jerking in his arms. Zero loved the feel of every ripple and clench of her cunt. The fire inside them was burning brighter than ever before.

He felt her getting closer to orgasm.

"That's it, baby. Let me hear you scream."

Prue cried out, screaming his name. Throughout her orgasm, he slammed inside her over and over again feeling the stirrings of his own orgasm.

Taking possession of her lips, Zero grunted as his release crashed through him. Tensing, he filled the condom with his cum, wishing it was inside her tight channel.

He collapsed on top of her, holding her tightly.

"Zero," she said, whispering his name.

"I know." He wasn't moving. Zero was holding onto her.

****

Zero's weight was bearable. Prue stroked his back feeling the heat of his breath on her neck. Closing her eyes, she tried to stop the thoughts and emotions that were building inside her. Life was a lot easier if she didn't give them time to manifest.

There were no promises or commitments, only one night of undeniable pleasure.

He pulled away first. She stared up at him as he looked down at her.

Fingers stroked her cheek then moved down to her lip. She opened her mouth, and he plunged a finger inside. Prue tasted her juices on his digit. Moaning, she sealed her mouth around the invading finger and sucked hard.

His cock kicked back into action.

She felt the jerk of his arousal inside her.

"I need to get rid of the condom. You're a fucking temptress." He removed his hand, dropping a kiss to her lips. "I'll be back."

Zero eased out of her body. The action made her wince. She hadn't fucked in such a long time. Unused muscles protested at being used once again after a long year of celibacy.

Prue watched him enter the bathroom. She heard the tap running followed by the flush of the toilet.

The line had been crossed. There was no going back to being simply friends.

Rolling over, she stared at the wall that faced her. There were no answers to her questions staring back at her.

Pushing hair off her face, she wondered what she was going to do when all this was over. For a few minutes she was able to forget about the threat to both of their lives. Right now, the reality of what they faced crashed inside her brain.

The bed dipped as he joined her. His arm banded around her waist, and he leaned in close kissing her neck. "Stop it," he said.

Jerking toward him, she stared into his eyes. "What?"

"Stop thinking about all the shit out there. Alan will wait. The fucked up shit he's got planned for us will wait another day. I've got you naked in my bed. I've just tasted and fucked your pussy. Life, right now, is good. Don't spoil it for shit in your head." He tightened his arm around her as she made to fight him.

"Let go of me."

"No."

They fought in the bed, but Prue was nowhere near as strong as Zero. He had her pressed to the bed. His large body was between her thighs as he held her hands beside her head. She wriggled, trying to get him off her. Nothing would budge him.

Exhausted, she remained still underneath him. Prue chose to glare at him instead.

"Are you done?" he asked.

"No."

"Then go ahead. Wriggle away. This is far more fun for me than it is you. I get to feel your body move underneath me." He pressed his hard cock against her pussy.

Moaning, she stopped. His cock was too inviting to resist.

"Now, I'm not going to do anything to you until you tell me what the fuck that was all about," he said.

"We … crossed … a … line." She spat each word at him, taking time to say them.

Zero's gaze landed on her. He didn't look confused or show any sign of misreading what she said. "The line was drawn by us, Prue. It can be knocked down by either one of us."

Her anger spiked. Fisting her palms, she wished she could slam it against his face.

"I will not be a notch on your bedpost or like some whore you use," she said.

He reared back, releasing her arms. She went to her elbows, but the rest of her was trapped by his large body. "Do I look like I'm treating you as some whore or a woman I'm only interested in having a good time with?" Zero looked angry. She'd seen him angry many times but never like this. "Any other woman I would take what I want and send her on her fucking way. I don't take time to linger with cuddles or talk. You're different, Prue. We're different."

Hope filled her at his words. They were different, but she always believed only she thought that way. When she heard about Sophia and saw the other woman, Prue knew she didn't stand a chance of competing.

Sophia was utterly feminine whereas Prue had grown up with Trevor and Zero. They taught her how to fight, shoot, play pool, and deal cards. She liked getting dirty under the hood of her car. Being a teacher was rewarding, and she loved her work. At the weekends it was her downtime where she got to do what she loved.

"You are not and will never be a notch on my bedpost. You mean too much to me."

"What about Sophia?"

"She was … a mistake. Since you've been here I haven't given her a thought, that's how unimportant she is to me. I don't even think about her. I care about her, but as Nash's woman and part of the club."

Don't let yourself hope.

Prue couldn't stop the new feelings invading her heart. She'd always loved Zero. He was her best friend. The guy she had grown up with and learned to depend upon. Only when she got older did her feelings deepen. She knew they would never be returned and so hadn't waited for him like some love-struck virgin. Prue lived her life without expecting anything from him in return.

"You fancied yourself in love with her," she said.

"Can't a man make a mistake?"

"You've changed your mind too quickly."

He smiled. "We were not going to do this, and yet we're here."

"This is different," she said.

"Why? Because you want to fuck whereas you don't want to trust me when I say I no longer love another woman?" he asked.

Zero had a point.

"What do you want me to do?" The words were hard to say. She was so used to being on her own. Zero visited her sporadically. She didn't have anyone in the world to trust or confide in. For ten years it had been her fighting for her life. It was nice being Prue once again. Ten years of being another woman hadn't been easy. There were times she didn't respond to the name Lilly.

"I want you to give me a chance, to give us a chance. I'm in this for the long haul," he said, touching her cheek. His finger ran across her lip.

She chuckled. The noise sounded hollow, and she didn't feel any humor.

"What's so funny?"

"You're saying this now, and yet Alan is intent on killing the both of us. We're not exactly going to have a long haul," she said, feeling depressed.

"Hey." He gripped her face, forcing her to look at him. "Alan is out there, and I can't promise you we will survive. What I will promise you is that I'll do everything in my power to keep us both alive. He's not going to win this fight. I won't let him."

"We can't stop him."

"Alan is a man. He's a man intent on revenge. I know what he's going through. I felt the same, and I did what I did. We know he's coming. He's going to strike, and we'll be ready." He caressed up her face, stroking her hair.

His touch soothed her.

"I can't help but feel we'll never be prepared for what Alan wants."

"He's crazy. Stop thinking about him and concentrate your pretty head on me. I'm not going to let him invade this moment. We'll do what we can, and we'll take care of what we can't." Zero leaned down, slamming his lips against hers.

The kiss started slow, and her thoughts were still taken by Alan. Zero soon took over. His tongue plundered her mouth as his hands stroked down her body.

Within minutes he had her panting, wanting his rock hard cock deep inside her.

"There she is." Zero pulled away. "I'm not finished with you tonight. All serious talk is banned. You try to talk serious and I will spank your ass so you can't sit for a week."

He leaned back, his hands going to her neck, feeling her pulse on either side.

Her heart was racing, and her pussy was soaking wet.

Need bloomed once again inside her, directed at Zero.

"Is your pussy wet for me?" he asked.

"Yes."

His hands moved down to cup her breasts. She felt his thumbs stroke across each nipple. "I love these tits. They're so ripe and full."

Zero moved down, taking her nipple into his mouth. She watched and heard him suck on the bud. When he bit down a pulse answered in her clit at the bite of pain. He soothed the pain by sliding his tongue over the burn.

He licked a path to her other breast and did the same, sucking, biting, and then licking.

Seconds later his hands moved down over her stomach and across her hips. He opened the lips of her sex and slid a finger through her clit. She gasped as he stroked the nub, sending her up off the bed.

"There, now that's the clit I love to play with. I've spent the last few weeks wondering what color your pussy hair would be. I knew you were a natural redhead, and seeing your color here turns me the fuck on," he said, pressing his thumb to her clit. He stroked across the hair covering her mound.

She gripped the sheets as he played with her.

"Watch me, Prue. Watch me play with your pussy."

Going to her elbows, she watched his fingers slide through her pussy. He used two fingers to stroke across her clit. It was hard to keep her eyes open as he teased her so intimately.

Biting her lip, she watched him go down, and one finger slid deep.

"Open them, Prue."

She hadn't been able to stop her eyes from closing.

"You're going to know who is playing with you."

Reaching out, she surrounded his length, pumping his shaft. Two could play at his game.

Chapter Ten

Batting her hands away, Zero climbed off the bed. He moved toward the furthest cabinet in his room and opened the bottom drawer.

"What are you doing?" she asked.

Seeing what he wanted, he glanced over his shoulder to look at her. "Do you trust me, Prue?"

She was silent, and he waited patiently for her answer.

"Why?"

"Do you trust me?" He wasn't going to give anything away. She had to give him an answer first.

"Yes, I trust you."

Going into his drawer he removed what he wanted. Turning back to her, he showed her what he'd picked.

"What the fuck do you think you're going to do with those?" she asked.

"I'm going to use them on you." He held a pair of fur lined cuffs.

She held her wrists close to her, shaking her head. "No, you're not cuffing me to this bed."

"I'll make it worth your while," he said.

Prue stared at the cuffs then at him. "How?"

"You'll be at my mercy, and you'll have to show me a great deal of trust." He held the cuffs with one finger through the link. "I've never used these on a woman. I was saving them for someone special."

"Sophia?"

"No, she never came to mind. Come on, Prue. Give yourself to me. Let me play a little." He took a step closer to the bed.

"You're not going to hurt me?" she asked.

He shook his head. "Everything I do to you,

you're going to like."

Once he stood at the headboard, he waited for her to cave. Only he owned the key. The door to his bedroom was locked, and he had no intention of sharing.

"Fine." She held her wrist out. Securing one cuff around her wrist, he looped the cuffs through the wooden head board and secured her second wrist. He gave a tug, happy with the fit. Prue wasn't going anywhere unless he released her.

"Now that is a sight to remember."

Zero wanted to take a picture, but he knew that was taking things too far too soon.

"Okay, you've got me locked up. What next?"

"You're at my mercy, to play with, to torture, and to fuck." He eased between her thighs, opening her legs wide to look at her glistening cunt. "You really are fucking sexy."

Sliding a finger through her wet heat, Zero moaned. She was burning him alive with her need.

Grabbing some pillows he eased them under her hips, opening her up. He lifted her legs to rest over his shoulders, staring down at her pussy. Using two fingers, he smeared them in her cream, coating them. Satisfied he eased his fingers to her ass. She jerked but didn't pull away as he pressed the tip to her puckered hole.

"What are you doing?" she asked.

"I'm playing. Your ass has been teasing me just as long as your pussy." He pressed the tip inside her ass feeling her muscles try to keep him out. She relaxed, and he slowly pressed forward feeling her quiver beneath his touch.

He added a second finger watching her take all of him. Her cunt leaked her cream out, dripping down the crease to her asshole.

"So fucking beautiful," he said. With his other

hand, he slid three fingers into her cunt. Even though he'd fucked her less than an hour ago she was still incredibly tight. Stretching her pussy then her asshole, he added a second finger, stretching her wide.

"Are you going to fuck my ass?"

"Not tonight. I'm only playing tonight. I will fuck your ass in time." Among her ass, pussy, and mouth, Zero knew he would be satisfied. Prue was insatiable. She responded to everything he gave her.

She whimpered as he thrust in and out of her ass with his fingers. Her cunt clenched down, keeping him inside her.

"That's it, baby, take me all."

"Please, Zero, I need your cock."

"I'll give it to you when I'm good and ready." Withdrawing from her pussy, he stroked his fingers through her slit, caressing her clit. He could spend hours touching her, loving her body. Her response was a thing of beauty.

In and out he pushed his fingers into her ass while stroking her clit with his other hand.

Prue squirmed, her body shaking with need. "Please," she said, begging.

Zero didn't respond and watched as her pussy grew wetter with his ministrations. When he could stand it no longer, he eased off the bed, going into the bathroom to wash his fingers. When he came back he found her sawing her legs together, clearly trying to gain friction that her legs wouldn't give her.

"Are you here to torture me?" she asked.

"A little. Don't worry, baby. I'll take care of all of your needs." Retrieving a condom, he tore into the foil and eased the rubber over his length. He gripped the base of his cock then stroked up to the tip. His touch was light so he wouldn't remove the rubber.

Her gaze was on his cock as he approached the bed. "I'll give you the fucking you need, baby."

Zero moved between her thighs, dropping a kiss to her precious jewel. Her scent invaded his senses, and he couldn't deny himself a taste of her cunt.

As he plunged his tongue into her heat, her cum exploded on his tongue.

She cried out, the screams echoing off the wall. Gripping her hips, he tugged her onto his tongue, spearing her pussy.

Prue called out his name over and over again. Moving up he sucked her clit into his mouth drinking her in.

He kissed up her body, biting onto her nipples until he claimed her mouth. She whimpered but opened her lips to take his invading tongue. Deepening the kiss, he gripped his shaft, sliding the tip through her creamy slit. He bumped her clit before going down to slide the tip into her pussy.

She glided her tongue over his, and their kiss deepened. He moaned, hands going to her hips as he thrust inside. Prue didn't stop her kiss, taking his cock and tongue into her body.

"That's it, baby, give me what I need," he said.

Zero filled her up, loving the feel of her tight cunt rippling around him. Breaking from the kiss, he stared into her captivating eyes. He loved looking into her eyes. They were always so expressive and gave him hope of there being something more between them.

Pulling out of her pussy, he slammed inside watching her cry out.

Over and over, he thrust into her waiting cunt, loving the noises coming from her. Glancing down to where they were joined he watched his latex covered cock pounding inside her pussy.

"Watch us together, Prue. Watch me fuck you and your pussy take my cock."

They were both panting for breath. Staring into her eyes, he saw her gaze was on his penetrating cock.

"You're so fucking beautiful. All I want to do is fuck you. I've got you trapped where I want you." The cuffs he'd placed around her wrists kept her in place. Leaning down, he sucked her nipple into his mouth, pulling the bud taut. When she screamed, arching up, he released her, flicking the tip with his tongue.

Holding onto her hips, he pounded inside her, never letting up as he fucked her hard and rough.

"Never going to get tired of fucking you," he said, slamming harder inside her.

Zero hit her cervix, and her face showed the pleasure and pain he was giving to her.

He caressed her clit, fucking her at the same time. Her tits bounced with the force of his thrusts, but he still didn't stop from fucking her. Zero wanted to brand her cunt with his name alone. Every time she thought about sex, he wanted his name to be on the tip of her tongue. No other man would ever know the pleasure of her body, only him. He would take care of her, love her, and give her everything her heart desired.

"You're so fucking beautiful."

She splintered apart in his arms. Her pussy squeezed the life out of his cock as she hurtled over the edge. Zero followed her into bliss, slamming his cock deep inside her. Once again he wished he was filling her up with his cum. Instead, he filled the condom collapsing over her as he finished. He held himself up on his arms, breathing against her neck.

Catching his breath, Zero knew there was nowhere else he wanted to be. Prue owned every part of him.

Glancing down into her closed eyes, he kissed her lips.

"There is no going back anymore," he said.

"I know."

"You're going to stay here and be with me."

"I can't just quit my job."

Running a hand over his face, he stared down at her. "Yeah, you can. There are jobs here, and if not, you can wait. I make more than enough money to keep us, Prue."

"I'm not living in the clubhouse. I wouldn't survive here."

"Then we'll get a house."

"Why are you not listening to me?" she asked.

"You're being difficult on purpose. I won't accept it. I'm not letting you go." He silenced her with his lips. Zero wasn't going to let her go.

****

Two hours later they were still arguing over where they were going to live and what they were going to do. They showered together, and she was no longer bound to the bed by his furry cuffs. She followed one of his tattoos as they argued.

"There are kids everywhere who need a good teacher," he said.

"I'm under contract."

"Then work your contract and come back here. Fort Wills is my life, Prue."

She sighed. He didn't know how tempted she was to give in and be with him. Half a night of fantastic sex and she was ready to cave.

"I've got a life as well." She had lived a mundane life that hadn't been exciting or thrilling in the past couple of months unless Zero called.

"I'm not disputing that." He covered her hands on

his chest. Flattening her palm on his chest, she glanced up at him. "You can't tell me you've had more fun back home alone than you have now."

Prue stayed silent resting her head on his chest.

"You've not played pool or had some fun. When was the last time you went shooting?" he asked.

"There's not a lot of call to go shooting."

Zero started talking, but she closed her eyes.

"Please, will you stop talking," she said. "I've not done anything because unlike you and Trevor, I never made friends easily. Playing pool, shooting, for me it was spending time with you guys. Doing it alone is just sad, depressing. So, no, I've not done anything fun, and you're right. The most fun I've had in a long time is with you." She leaned up, opening her eyes to stare at his lips. "Can we not talk about the future until after Alan is gone?"

"You don't want to make plans in case he kills one of us."

She nodded. "The last thing I want to do is build my hopes up when there is a good chance we could be burying one if not both of us."

"I'm not going to spank your ass for bringing him up. I did the same. We will be having this discussion again," he said, pushing some hair behind her ear.

Prue smiled. "Do you promise that?"

"Yes, I fucking do."

He ran his thumb over her lip, and she moaned.

"I had no idea it could be like this," she said.

"Me neither." He withdrew his hand, and she missed his touch.

"You've fucked plenty of women. You've never experienced this with any of them." She looked at him.

"No. They've been women, and they all meant nothing. Not like you."

"Good answer." She smiled and then pressed her lips to his.

"I've got plenty of good answers for you."

"Go on then, charm me." She rested her chin on her hands.

"Your tits are the nicest I've ever had the pleasure of sucking," he said.

She chuckled. "Very romantic. You'll be winning awards and have women knocking down your door to get to you." She rolled her eyes, waiting for him to continue.

"This is my version of romance. You want flowers and false promises, get a book. This is real. I'm real." He stroked her cheek with his knuckles. "I love the feel of your pussy wrapped around my cock. I like the way you get wet from my touch. You're not afraid to take your pleasure. It's not just me fucking you. You're fucking me as well. We're there together for the pleasure. Your body drives me crazy. I don't know what to do half of the time. You're so fucking beautiful."

Prue loved his compliments. She could listen to them all day long.

"It's not just your body that drives me crazy, it's your mind. You're not afraid to speak your thoughts, but it's stuff I want to know and listen to. You don't always think of yourself." He smiled, and her breath caught at the sight. "You like playing pool and getting your hands dirty. What you see as a lack in your character I see as a bonus. You're not afraid to be yourself. When I'm with you, I don't think you're putting on a show."

"I'd never put on a show," she said.

"There, that is some of what I like about you. They're what I consider your charms."

"I like it."

She sat up and straddled his hips. His cock lay flaccid against his stomach. "I love your cock," she said, running her fingers up and down his chest.

His thick arms moved to her legs.

"I love everything about you, Zero," she said.

"Do you love me, baby?"

"That will be something you'll have to find out."

Zero cupped her ass, squeezing the cheeks together. Prue moaned, thrusting her chest out. He sat up, claiming one nipple in his mouth.

Sinking her fingers into his hair, she tugged on the strands, pulling him away from her breast.

"I'm in charge now." She shoved him back to the bed, climbing off his body. Standing beside the bed, she gripped his hardening cock. "And I want to play."

Prue worked his length, getting him hard once again. She couldn't believe how easy it was to get him ready. Zero was a sex machine. When she thought it was going to be their last round of sex, he would get hard again.

"Are you going to suck my cock, Prue?" he asked. His hands rested underneath his head.

"We'll see." Working his cock from root to tip she watched his pre-cum build and leak out of the tiny slit at the head.

Arousal gripped her hard at the sight of his shaft. She knew what kind of pleasure he could give, and she wanted to feel him pounding away inside her once again.

His hand slid down the outside of her thigh. "Move up here."

She didn't argue. Zero knew how to give her pleasure, and she wasn't prepared to stop any kind of pleasure she could get. Stepping closer, she opened her thighs as he skimmed his fingers up the inside of her thigh. He teased her with his touch. There was nothing she could do to force him.

Prue stroked his shaft, moving down to cup his

heavy balls.

"I can smell your cunt from here. You're always on fire." His palm cupped her pussy, and she groaned, closing her thighs around his hand. "Don't even think of keeping me away from your sweet pussy, baby. This is my pussy."

Opening her thighs, his finger slid through her slit.

Tease him.

Taking hold of his cock, she leaned over his body, circling the tip of his cock with her tongue.

"Fuck!" He cursed, hissing the word out into the air. Smiling around his cock, she stroked his length, taking as much of him into her mouth as she could. "You're a fucking tease."

Two fingers slammed inside her. She met the thrusts, wanting him to make it burn.

Whack!

His palm slapped her ass cheek, making her yelp. She loved the sting and wriggled her ass for more.

"You want more, baby?"

She nodded, taking him to the back of her throat. When she was about to gag on his length, she pulled away. Flicking the tip, she cried out as another slap to her ass and the thrust of his fingers drove her wild. No longer able to hold back her need, Prue took his cock into her mouth. She bobbed her head on his length, groaning as the pleasure increased.

"Fuck! Suck my cock, baby. Let me feel you swallow it." He thrust his hips up to her waiting mouth. Keeping her mouth open, she took as much of him as possible.

When her orgasm slammed into her, she swallowed down the tip no longer caring about gagging.

Zero growled, driving into her mouth. Her

orgasm subsided, and Prue moved off his hands.

With shaking hands, she tore into the foil packet, removed the latex and slid it over his rock hard cock. It took her several attempts to get the condom on his cock.

He took over, placing the rubber over himself. Straddling his hips, she held onto his cock and slid it along her slit before taking him into her body. Both of them cried out at the same time as she sank onto his length.

"So fucking tight," he said, gripping her hips.

She drew his hands up her body to tease her breasts. He took over, working the buds with his fingers until they were rock hard, pressing against his palm.

Putting her hands on his chest, she rode his cock, slapping her body down onto him, taking him deep. From this angle, he felt bigger than ever before. Her pussy was filled by his length creating the dual sensation of pleasure and pain.

Together, they fucked hard. Prue screamed as Zero took over, grabbing her hips and forcing her to take more of him.

"Fuck," he said again. "I'm going to come."

Prue rode him, feeling her own release close.

They came together. Their combined pleasure rode the other to completion. When it was over, she collapsed over him not wanting to move.

"We're perfect for each other, Prue."

In that moment, she couldn't argue.

Chapter Eleven

One week later

Zero wrapped the wire around his arm as he glanced toward the playground where the kids were playing with Prue. They'd been having sex for well over a week, and Zero couldn't get enough of her. This morning he walked into the pantry to see her ass in the air as she bent over to look at something. He'd never seen a more tempting view in his life. Closing the door, he lifted her dress up, tore her panties aside, opened a condom and was inside her in less than a minute. Each time he was with her, it felt like the first time all over again. The chemistry never diminished even when they argued. In fact, fucking Prue after they argued was as hot as when they didn't.

The lockdown was getting old, and he was waiting for Alan to make his next move. It was next to impossible to live when you were worried about an old foe.

"You're in love," Butch said, coming to stand beside him.

"What?" He turned to his friend seeing the smile on Butch's lips. Out of all of them, Butch knew how to sneak out of the compound every night to visit his woman. Zero didn't know who she was, but she had to be special to risk Tiny's wrath. Alex hadn't found anything out other than what Zero already knew and had told them.

"You can't take your eyes off each other. Also, I heard you two going at it this morning. You're always fucking. I walked into the pool room the other day, and you were fucking each other."

Zero chuckled, recalling the way he'd used the

pool room.

"Are you jealous?"

"No. I'm just pleased Nash is not ready to murder you. He can relax as you're taken by another woman."

Yeah, he was able to be in Sophia's company without fear of losing a limb or something more important to him.

"It's nice not thinking about a woman I can't have. I don't want her anymore."

"How do you know?" Butch asked.

"I've always loved Prue. She was one of my best friends, and over the years it has changed. Being with her, she lifts my world. She makes me yearn for a family of our own." Zero knew Trevor would give his blessing. They were good together, and it would always be like that between them.

"I'm happy for you, brother. I hope we can deal with this shit and get over it soon." Butch slapped him on the back before leaving Zero to finish what he was doing. Lash and Angel were talking together with their son on Lash's hip.

Turning his attention back to Prue, he made his way over to her, draping the wire over the bike. Wrapping his arms around her waist, he pulled her close. His cock hardened at the feel of her plump, inviting ass against his cock.

"What do you think you're doing?" she asked, giggling.

"I'm touching my woman."

She moaned, turning her head enough for him to kiss her lips.

"I want your cock," she said, whispering the words against his lips.

"You'll get me tonight. I'm going to fuck you so hard. Your pussy is going to be sore in the morning."

Prue wriggled her ass, rubbing his cock. "I can't wait."

He held her for several minutes basking in the feel of truly possessing her. They hadn't talked about her going back home or of her moving closer to him.

"I love this," she said.

She hadn't told him how she felt, but he believed she loved him. Zero was in love with her and had been for a long time. He just hadn't realized it. His guilt over Trevor had held him back, and he'd found solace in loving Sophia from afar. Over the years he'd tortured himself, stopping him from having any other woman.

"I'll leave you to take care of the kids," he said, kissing her head.

Prue nodded, moving away to push the swing.

He made his way into the clubhouse, picking up the toolbox stored in Tiny's office. Zero knocked on the door even though it was partially open. Tiny had a tendency to fuck Eva, and if any of them walked in the leader made sure to hurt them when he finally got hold of them.

"Come in," Tiny said.

Opening the door, he found the office empty apart from Tiny sitting at the computer. He was clicking away when Zero entered.

"I'm here for the toolbox," Zero said.

"It's in the corner." Tiny glanced up at him as Zero retrieved the box. "How are you and Prue holding up?"

"We're doing okay. Waiting for Alan to strike is not helping matters."

"I know. Nothing has happened at all. It's like he doesn't exist. I'm sick and tired of chasing ghosts." Tiny sat back, rubbing a hand over his face.

"Nothing from Alex and Ned?"

"No. Alan was there, and then he was gone. We'll find him. Everyone slips up eventually."

"What if he doesn't?" Zero asked.

"Then we better hope we're ready for the fight he's going to give us."

Zero stared down at the ground. He hated feeling helpless. Ten years ago he'd fucked up, and now the whole club was paying the price for his fucking stupidity.

"What's the matter?" Tiny asked, leaning back in his chair to stare at him.

"I'm sorry. I was such a fucking idiot. I didn't even think about what was happening or the consequences." Zero stopped talking. What could he say?

"You took matters into your own hands. Trevor, your friend, you were close?" Tiny got up from his chair, moving around the desk to sit on the edge.

"Yeah, we were like brothers. I wanted him to join The Skulls. He had other plans."

"Plans that got him killed."

Zero nodded. "Yeah."

"Look, you were a prospect ten years ago. We fuck up, and we learn from our mistakes. I can't turn around and say you shouldn't have fucked over this guy because I don't know what I'd do if it was a friend of mine." Tiny let out a sigh. "I've buried a lot of friends, and I've killed a lot of people. I know if anyone fucks with my family, they will die. You were taking care of your family, and you were hurt. You fucked up and left the man alive." Tiny shrugged. "I can rant and rave at you, but in the end, I'd be a hypocrite. I will hurt and kill anyone who thinks they can take my family away from me. I expect the same from all my men."

"Okay."

"You can beat yourself up, or you can brush this shit off and deal with the now rather the then, got it?" Tiny asked.

"Yeah, I got it."

"Good. Stop being a pussy and go work."

Zero headed to the door.

"Next time you want to fuck your woman, do so away from the pantry. Watching your ugly ass is not a sight I'm going to forget easily. It's there."

Laughing, Zero left the room, feeling happier than he had in a long time. Tiny didn't hold him responsible, and knowing that helped him to deal with what he had done. He stood outside watching Prue with the children. Making his way toward his bike, he started working. He pulled the bike away from the others in the center of the compound near the gate. The gate was not open, but Zero wasn't afraid.

He set to work, listening to the sounds of the children laughing. Life was good. Working on his bike he could pretend for several minutes that nothing was wrong. Every time he looked at the closed gate he was reminded of the danger that surrounded them.

"Angel, no!" Lash shouting the two words drew Zero up. He turned in time to see Angel standing in front of him, looking panicked. In the next second gun shots rang out.

Eyes widening he watched Angel jerk and fall.

Pain burst through his body as two shots filled him. Collapsing to the floor he fell in a way where he saw Angel. Her eyes were closed as she lay on the ground. The gate was opened as men ran out following.

Screams, shouts, cries rent the air.

Zero stared at Angel's face. Was she breathing? From where he lay he saw she'd taken three in the back.

"Take him, get him away from here," Lash said, dropping down beside Angel. "Baby, what the fuck did you do?"

The pain and anguish inside Lash were easy to hear.

"Zero, oh no, someone call an ambulance, quickly," Prue said. She rolled him over, and he looked up at her. "You can't die. Do you hear me? You can't die."

"Angel, fucking answer me," Lash said, shouting.

He heard sirens coming. They had to get here to save Angel.

"I love you," he said, looking up at Prue. Her beautiful face was a sight to behold. Reaching up, he touched her cheek and frowned. His fingers were covered in blood.

"No, you're not going to die on me. You can't. I'll be all alone. I love you, Zero." She dropped her head to his. "You promised me."

Fuck, he needed to fight.

If Angel was dead, Lash would never survive it. He couldn't believe the other woman had stepped in front of him. She'd taken a bullet.

Sending prayers, he hoped she survived.
****

Prue sat in the ambulance with Zero as they made their way to the hospital. Angel was with Lash in the other. Glancing out of the window she saw Tiny and the club was following. From what she heard the other man had organized for the prospects to stay in the clubhouse with the women.

Zero had passed out, but she held his hand tightly. When the ambulance came to a stop, she stayed out of the way, watching them take the cart inside.

Screams, yells, and the sound of destruction were coming from inside the hospital. Angel and Lash had arrived a few minutes before.

Entering the hospital she saw two security guards

were slumped against the wall. Nurses were trying to reason with Lash. The cold fury on his face was clear to see.

"Sir, you've got to let us do our job."

"No, she's my fucking wife. I go with her." Lash picked up a chair and threw it against the reception. People moved out of the way. Prue stayed well back knowing she was no match against Lash's strength.

Tiny ran into the hospital followed by Nash and Killer. All three men grabbed Lash as the other man fought.

"You need to stand down," Tiny said.

"No, she was shot three fucking times. Three times in the back, Tiny. I need to be in there with her."

"Lash, you're not a doctor. You can't do anything to help her. You're useless. How can you help when she needs a professional to take care of her wounds?" Nash asked.

None of their words were getting through. Lash was breaking apart, shattering before their eyes. His woman was hurt, and there was nothing he could do.

Tears filled Prue's eyes at the pain.

The men hadn't secured his feet. Lash kicked his brother in the nuts, and Nash fell. Next Killer was thrown off easily. Tiny held on tight while the other men scrambled to help. A doctor walked into the room holding a syringe. Placing a hand to her lips, she watched as he got close. While Lash was fighting, the doctor approached from behind and struck Lash. The other man tore away, ready to do damage.

Prue stayed still as Lash suddenly slumped on the ground calling Angel's name. When he was out, Tiny and the others helped him onto a bed, and they wheeled him out.

"Fuck, this is bad," Nash said.

She followed the men outside as Tiny cursed, kicking over his bike.

This was not good when Tiny lost his mind. It had to be Alan. He was the only one who could attack them like this.

"Lash will not come back from this if he loses Angel," Nash said.

"I know."

Biting her lip, she tucked some hair behind her ear seeing Zero's blood on her hands. Fuck, when did she have his blood on her hands?

"She wasn't moving, Tiny. Three bullets to the back, this is something she might not be coming back from." Killer spoke up this time.

"I need to call Devil."

Prue left them alone and went to the bathroom to try to clean the blood of her hands. She felt sick to her stomach at the sight of blood. Tears filled her eyes as she entered the bathroom, and she let them go. Staring in the mirror she saw them run down her cheeks. Soaping her hands, she placed them under the hot water trying to wash away the blood.

Over and over she scrubbed her hands.

The bathroom door opened, and Nash stood looking in. "We were worried about you," Nash said.

"I'm washing blood off my hands. Zero's blood." She bit her lip, wiping the tears away with the back of her hand.

"He's still in surgery."

"I know. I didn't imagine it would be quick." She scrubbed her hands, trying her best to remove all evidence of Zero's blood. Alan had won. This was going to ruin the club if either Zero or Angel died.

"Hey, don't start losing it yet. We're all still fighting here."

"How can you be so calm?" she asked, drying her hands on some towel. "Your brother's wife is in surgery. She was shot in the back three times by a maniac trying to ruin Zero. We're in the hospital again. Tell me how you're calm?"

"The battle is not over. Angel is in the hospital, and she went into that hospital room alive. Zero doesn't have life threatening wounds. He will come out of this alive. The time for panicking is not now. My brother needs me to be strong." Nash stepped into the bathroom. The tears were falling thick and fast down her cheeks.

"I saw it. I saw the car drive past. The bullets and I saw them hit Angel. They waited for her to fall before aiming for Zero. None of them had any intention of stopping." She sobbed the words out as Nash wrapped his arms around her.

"He's going to get through this. Zero is strong. Stronger than any of us realize," Nash said.

"I can't handle him dying on me."

"No one is dying," Tiny said, standing in the room. "Devil is calling me back. I need you to stay out here, Prue, and keep an eye on Lash and get word to me on Angel and Zero. Can you do that?"

She nodded. "Yes, I can do that."

"Good, we need you. The club needs you."

Stepping away from Nash, she followed Tiny out of the bathroom toward the waiting area. Taking a seat on one of the chairs, she watched the clear doors. Not long ago Zero had been waiting to hear news about her. Now their roles were reversed as she watched the doors like a mad woman. Lash would be out for a few hours. She hoped they had news by the time he woke up.

Killer sat beside her, groaning as he did. "I spend more time sitting on my ass in this fucking hospital than I do anything else."

She smiled, even though she didn't know what there was to be happy about.

"I know you're freaking out over what's happening and don't want to know anything other than if Zero and Angel are going to be all right," he said.

Turning toward him, she waited for him to finish.

"What I'm saying is I've been here a lot. I was here with Kelsey when she tried to kill herself and other times. Fuck, this doesn't sound good at all."

"Why don't you just make your point?" she said, shaking.

"We've been to hell and back again, and yet we're still here. Kelsey is my wife, and she's pregnant with our first child. We're all surviving."

"What if this will be the one time they don't?" she asked.

"I don't allow myself to think or feel that way. Once you let the bad in, you can't think of the good." He tapped her hand. "Try to think positive about everything that is happening here."

She nodded, watching him leave. Tiny was on the phone, and she watched him talking. Tears were streaking down his face.

After a couple of hours the doctor came out to tell her news. She listened, as did The Skulls as they were told Zero was fine. The bullets were easy to remove, and he'd be on his feet within the next forty-eight hours. Prue was thankful.

Angel was not doing as well. One of the bullets was next to her spine. Extracting the bullet with precision took time. Any wrong move and she might never walk again. Two of the bullets had been removed, and they didn't know the extent of the damage. They were taking tests and observing the damage during surgery.

Prue sent up a prayer for the sweet woman. Alan

was going to die, and she was going to make sure he hurt and would watch him die before she left his dead body. Running a hand down her face, she left the reception to go and see Lash.

He lay on the bed, which looked like it was going to collapse from his weight. The pain on his face was clear even in sleep.

Prue walked up to his bed side. She took his hand and couldn't find the strength to smile.

"I'm sorry."

The words were filled with much feeling, but she knew it didn't matter to him what she said. If Angel didn't make it out of this hospital alive, Lash would do everything in his power to hurt the one responsible.

Alan had won this round like he'd won the other two. Leaving Lash's side, she made her way out of his room to wait for more news. Zero was going to survive, and now it was the wait to see about Angel.

****

Jumping up and down giddy at what he'd done, Alan stared at the room. Putting a cross through Angel's picture and another through Lash, he giggled. The pain had been clear from that split second he got to see. Lurking in the shadows, he watched the car approach, his men fire and the ensuring chaos.

His plans were not over. He doubted Zero would stay in the hospital.

Circling Sophia's head, he pocketed a knife

Lockdown was over, and the game could truly begin.

Chapter Twelve

"Devil has arrived in town. He's at the clubhouse getting caught up with Alex, who made it back into town," Tiny said.

Zero listened to his leader, his president, talk as he lay in bed with Prue sat beside him. The conversation being directed at him was not what he wanted to hear. Seeing Prue since waking up had been the highlight of his morning. The drugs they fed him kept him out of it for some time. He couldn't feel a single thing. If it wasn't for seeing the wounds covered by bandages, Zero wouldn't believe he was actually shot.

"What happened to Angel?" he asked, cutting across Tiny.

The fact Lash wasn't in his room and neither was Nash didn't fill him with confidence.

Please, don't let that woman, that angel, die for trying to protect me.

He closed his eyes, seeing her hands reaching up to push him out of the way. Before she even touched him, the bullets had hit her.

"What do you want to know?" Tiny asked.

Prue's hand tightened inside his, locking their fingers together tightly.

"I want to know if she's alive. She tried to protect me. I need to know that she's okay," he said, gritting his teeth. Tears filled his eyes, and he scrubbed them away.

"She's alive," Tiny said.

"Then what are you not telling me?"

He saw Tiny and Prue look at each other.

"Tell me, goddamn it. I need to know what else this bastard has done," Zero said.

"She's in a coma, and the doctors don't know when she's going to wake up." Prue stopped, hesitating.

"What else? Give it all to me," Zero said.

"They don't know if she'll be able to walk once she wakes up. They removed the bullet with minimal damage. We don't know what will happen once she wakes up. She could walk again or need some physiotherapy to walk again or she may never walk again."

He squeezed Prue's hand. "Is Lash with her?" he asked.

"Yes."

Zero tugged the wires out of him that hooked him up to the machines.

"You can't leave your bed," Prue said.

"I will do whatever the hell I want to do." Zero sat up in bed, grunting with the movement. Several nurses ran into the room trying to stop him. Ignoring them, he stood up. "Tiny, I'm going to see Lash and the woman who tried to save my life. Tell them to back the fuck off before I end up in prison."

Tiny shouted out for them to leave him alone. Standing tall, Zero held onto Prue and made his way out of the room. He felt a little dizzy and gripped onto the wall for stability.

"Your ass is showing," she said.

"I don't give a fuck. There will be no more fun until Alan is fucking dead."

They walked down the long corridor, and he was starting to have doubts about going to thank Lash.

When they walked into a room he was more than thankful for the respite. Prue dumped him into the closest chair. The drugs they'd given him were a fucking strong combination. Lash was sitting beside Angel, who was hooked up to several machines. Nash stood in the corner of the room with Sophia beside him.

"Come on, baby. You need to wake up. I need

you. Our son needs you." Lash kept talking, stroking his fingers up her arm. "Wake up and I'll take us away for a long summer vacation. You want to go to Italy, we'll go."

The pain in Lash's voice tore at Zero.

"Come on, wake up."

Sophia was sobbing in the corner.

"I'm sorry," Zero said.

Lash jerked around to look at him. "Are you all right?"

"Yes, she will pull through." Zero nodded toward Angel. He wouldn't accept anything other than her making it through.

"She will. Tiny has agreed to let us go for the summer. I promised her on our honeymoon that I would take her to Italy. I'm going to make sure she gets everything her heart desires." Lash was stroking her blonde hair off her head.

Silence fell in the room for several minutes.

"I don't blame you," Lash said, turning to look at him.

A lump formed in the back of his throat. "Why? If it wasn't for me this wouldn't be happening."

"You did what you did. Blaming you will not change what's happening." Lash wiped the tears off his face. "The fucker will pay for what he's done."

Zero looked at Lash feeling the anger consume him. "I will bring you the bastard's head."

Alan had been controlling this game for so long. It was time to take a little back for themselves.

"Good."

Zero stayed inside Lash and Angel's room for several minutes. On his way out he saw Devil was making his way toward the room. As they passed each other the older man reached out, touching his shoulder.

"We'll kill the bastard. Tiny told me everything that happened. He will die."

Nodding, Zero made his way back to his room with Prue by his side. She fussed around his bed, putting his wires back where they came. "I didn't know you were a nurse." She hooked up each machine to the pad. The needle he'd pulled out, stopping the morphine, Prue called the nurse to come and replace.

"All night I've stared at these machines. I remembered where they went."

The nurse walked into the room replacing the morphine.

Sitting in the bed, he waited for the pain to lessen.

"Stop walking around the room. Come and lie with me." He patted the bed, moving over to give her room.

"I was so scared. I thought I lost you," she said, lying down beside him.

"It takes a lot to take me out." He wrapped his arm around her waist, pulling her close. Her lemony scent invaded his senses. "I can rest knowing you're beside me."

Kissing her neck, Zero waited for her to ask the question he would bet was right on her lips.

"Go on, ask me, baby," he said, waiting patiently.

"You told me you loved me."

"I know." Staring at her face, he waited for her to look at him.

"Do you love me?" she asked.

"With all my heart. Do you love me?"

"Yes, I've loved you for a long time." She turned to him, stroking his face. "I'll be with you."

"What? You want to move to Fort Wills?"

"I'll move to Fort Wills. I'll stay by your side and love you, support you."

Linking their fingers together, he pushed some of her red hair away from her face.

"I'm going to hold you to that." He leaned forward, taking her lips.

"Alan?"

"Will die. He's a scarred man intent on revenge." Staring up at the ceiling, Zero searched for the right words. "He's not a ghost. Alan's like any man. We've just got to wait for him to take what he wants."

"You're not afraid?" she asked.

"I'm afraid of many things. I've got something to fight for. I've got you back in my life. Taking out Angel was his biggest mistake," he said. "We're going to fight back."

"You need to get well first."

"I'll be out of here by tomorrow. I'm not waiting around. Alan is going to strike again while we're all panicking."

"How do you know?" she asked.

"It's what I'd do. You're intent on revenge and want one person to suffer in particular, you strike hard." Zero rubbed his eyes, wondering who he was going to hit out at next.

"You don't seem scared of him anymore," she said.

"He's made his move, and I'm waiting for him to make his demands."

Prue rolled to her side, staring him in the face. "Do you think he intended to hurt Angel?"

"I've no idea. It had to have been a stroke of luck for him to get her and—" Zero stopped, frowning. "He told you he was going to take pleasure in my pain. Why would shooting at the compound give him pleasure? He couldn't have been the shooter. The car was moving too fast for him to be there," he said, trying to work out where his thoughts were going.

"He was waiting around, watching what was happening," she said.

"Get Tiny. I need to talk to him." He watched Prue leave the room, and he sat up. Alan had to have been in the background watching.

Running a hand down his face, he felt tired with all the shit.

Prue entered the room with Tiny and Devil.

"Do we have security across the street?" he asked.

"We've got security around the outside of the compound," Tiny said.

"Get Whizz to look through the tapes. You're looking for a man lurking in the shadows, possibly wearing a hooded jacket." Zero reached over for some water.

"You think he's going to be that close?" Devil asked.

"His intention is to make me suffer and for me to realize how much he can make me suffer. Why attack if he's not going to get the pleasure in seeing it?" Zero asked.

"He has a point," Devil said.

"We'll get back to the clubhouse. Eva's waiting for us. I've left Butch, Blaine, and Steven to keep an eye on everything. They'll keep you protected."

Zero nodded.

"I'm staying with him," Prue said, sitting on the side of the bed.

"I don't think we've had the pleasure of an introduction," Devil said, stepping forward.

"Back the fuck off." Zero shot the other man a glare.

"Please, I'm a happily married man. Lexie would

cut my dick off if she found out I touched another woman. My cock is branded for her and her alone," Devil said. "Even Lash's blonde woman won't tempt me away from my woman."

Zero kept his gaze on him. "This is Prue. Prue, this is Devil. He's the leader of Chaos Bleeds and a friend to The Skulls."

"It's nice to meet you," she said, shaking the other man's hand.

Once the introductions were over, he watched Devil and Tiny leave.

"A bit possessive, weren't you?" she asked.

"You don't know Devil. The man loves women. I'm surprised he's settled down into marriage." Wrapping his arms around her, Zero held onto his woman, knowing he would do everything to keep her safe.

****

Prue helped put Zero's jacket on. The nurses and doctors were trying to convince him to stay. He refused. Nothing she said helped either. He was leaving the hospital today.

"We can wait to take Alan out," she said.

"I can't wait. He's out there, and I can't stay here waiting for him to strike again."

Nurses and doctors charged past their door going into the main reception. "We've got a code red, a stabbing," one of the nurses said as they passed.

Frowning, Prue looked at her watch seeing it was gone ten. Tiny was supposed to be coming to collect them.

"It's all go in the hospital," Zero said, wincing.

"It's where a lot of people come to get fixed." She ran her hands down his arms, letting out a sigh. "I wish none of this had happened, but at the same time I'm glad it has. I'm such an awful person."

He grabbed her arm and pulled her around to face him.

"If this hadn't happened I wouldn't be here with you," she said, cupping his face, brushing her lips against his.

Zero stroked her cheek. "We'd have gotten there eventually. I love you, baby."

She went to her toes and kissed his lips.

Someone cleared his throat, and they turned. Her stomach turned over as she caught sight of Tiny. He was covered in blood.

"What the hell has happened?" Zero asked, holding her tighter than ever before.

"Sophia's been stabbed. She went to take the trash out and didn't come back in. Nash found her on the ground, bleeding out," Tiny said. "I was helping Sandy trying to stop the blood flow."

She glanced up at Zero. His face was pale as he looked at Tiny.

"This shit needs to end," Tiny said. "Whizz is going to meet a friend. We looked over the tapes." He opened his jacket withdrawing a picture. "Whizz has got a guy who has the ability to tap into security footage and compare the identities. We didn't have a picture. He's got to go and meet him outside of Fort Wills. The last I spoke to him, Whizz is waiting for the guy to show up."

Prue took the picture off him and saw Alan in the shadows.

"This is him."

"Whizz is trying to locate where he is and really thinks his contact can help."

Zero nodded. "How is Nash?"

"Crazy right now. He's, he's not in a good position with all of this," Tiny said. "I've got to go."

She watched Tiny leave the room. Looking up at her man she saw he was pale. "Do you need to sit down?"

"I'm not in love with her, Prue. Don't start thinking this has anything to do with you. Sophia didn't deserve to be attacked because of me. He's attacking everyone, and she mentioned she was expecting a baby." He took her hand, drawing her knuckles to his lips. "I swear, I love you."

Caressing his cheek, she brushed her lips against his cheek.

"I love you." She didn't completely believe him.

"Do you believe me?" he asked, tucking some hair behind her ear.

"No, I don't." She answered him honestly.

"I know it's going to take me a lifetime to prove my love, and I'll do it." He tugged her close, and she had no choice but to sit on his lap. "When you were hurt, I didn't want to leave the hospital. You being killed would hurt me more than anything. I can't live without you."

She caressed his hands where they covered her stomach. "I love you, Zero."

Resting her head against him, she closed her eyes.

"You own my heart." They stayed on the bed until Nash walked into the room. He was pale. His shirt was covered in blood, and his eyes were bloodshot.

"I want to hurt him, and I want to hurt you. I know she's been targeted because of you, but you're my brother and I know your heart lies elsewhere," Nash said.

Prue's eyes filled with tears at the anguish on his face.

"I will not raise a daughter alone. You will find this fucker, and you will kill him. Ten years ago you started something, and now you're going to finish it, or I swear to God, Zero, I will end you."

Tiny was standing behind the other man.

"I'm sorry," Zero said.

She felt him tense up, and she stared at Nash knowing his words meant nothing to him.

"I don't give a fuck about what you've got to say. The only way to make this up to me is by getting this fucker and hurting him." Nash turned to Tiny. "There, I've said my piece."

"We're a club, Nash. The club takes care of its own," Tiny said.

Prue saw the other man was tense ready to hold Nash back.

"It's easy for you to say. Eva is still safe with your kids." Nash spoke the words with a sneer.

"Zero accepted you back even though you were fucking high. You took drugs and risked the safety of the whole fucking club. You almost killed Eva when you were fucking high," Tiny said. "You want to fight, then you can fight afterward. Right now, we band the fuck together and fight this new enemy." Tiny reached out pushing Nash against the wall. "Am I fucking clear?"

"Crystal fucking clear," Nash said.

"You want to leave the club, tell me now. We're in this together. I'm here for you all. I'm not going to let you fuck up a club brother because your woman is fighting for her life. We handle our battles when everyone is safe."

Zero's hands tightened around her.

"I don't want to leave the club. I want to get to my woman. Can I leave now?" Nash asked.

Several seconds passed before Tiny let the other man go. She watched Nash leave without another word.

Tiny let out a sigh. "You're going to need to bring the men proof Alan's dead."

"I will."

"Wow, I thought my club was full of fucking drama," Devil said. "You guys are fucking magnets for trouble."

"Shut the fuck up, Devil," Tiny said.

Zero held her tightly.

"We're not leaving yet." Tiny ran fingers through his hair. "Everything is so fucked up. We're staying to make sure Sophia is okay."

"How is Angel?" Prue asked.

"Still in a coma. The doctors are hopeful that she'll wake up soon." Tiny paced the room, looking at the bottom of the bed.

"We'll stay here. Will you give us an update on what's happening to Sophia?" Zero asked.

"Yes."

Seconds later they were alone. The room was deadly silent. She got up from his lap and closed the door to their room. Opening the bathroom door she checked to make sure it was clear.

"Alan lurks everywhere. He's a fucking nightmare." She folded her arms over her chest, staring at her man. "So, I, you, and Angel have been shot. He tortured and killed the nurse you slept with. Sophia is more personal and been stabbed. Is this some kind of pattern?"

Zero turned on the bed to face her. "I don't know. I stabbed him multiple times, and I sure as fuck hurt him."

She saw him look down at the picture they had of him lurking in the shadows.

"Why wait ten years?" he asked.

"You fucked him up. It takes time to mend broken bones. You don't know the extent of the damage you inflicted. He's been waiting and mending himself," Prue said. She had thought long and hard about why Alan was waiting 'til now.

"He can hurt the whole of the club before he gives up." Zero put the picture on the bed, returning his attention back to her.

"Do you really think he's not going to get bored until all of us are dead?"

"I really don't know. This is more than I thought he was capable of," Zero said.

"Where do you think he's going to go next?" she asked, stepping closer.

He took her hand tugging her closer. Zero rested his hands on her hips, staring into her eyes.

"What?"

"I don't have an answer for what he's going to do next. You cannot leave my side, do you hear me? I will not sacrifice you to him."

She kissed his palm. "I'm not going anywhere. I will fight him by your side."

Wrapping her arms around his neck, she breathed in his masculine scent. This moment wasn't going to last long. Alan had a plan, and right now they were working to his plan, no one else's.

"Trevor would be so pissed off right now," Zero said.

Withdrawing, she frowned at him. "Why?"

"He would hate how we're being given the runaround by a man we don't even know that well. All of our lives we've handled everything thrown our way, and yet we don't have a clue when Alan is going to strike next."

She rubbed at her temple. "What are you trying to say?"

"We've been looking at this all fucking wrong. Alan is scared." He pointed at the picture. "He doesn't want anyone to remember he was around. The guy is trying to be a fucking ghost."

"I don't see what you're trying to say."

Zero stood up, grunting. "Fuck, he's going to be in one of the Fort Wills abandoned warehouses. The only place he can go without being detected. No one goes to those places. Fuck, we own one of the warehouses because it's secure. We've just got to figure out which one and take him out."

Prue smiled seeing what he was saying. They could stop Alan before he had a chance to lash out and hurt the people they cared about.

****

"So you're the computer whizz. You type everything into a little computer, and pop, there is a wealth of information at your fingertips?" Alan stared into Whizz's eyes. The man was tied to a chair, his arms bound to the arms of the chair as his feet were also tied to the chair to stop him from moving.

"What the fuck do you want with me?" Whizz asked, cursing.

Stepping back, Alan looked at the board of pictures he'd made of The Skulls. After Sophia had been taken away, he'd gotten his men to follow Whizz. They had watched him waiting near a dirt road on the outside of Fort Wills. The opportunity to take him was irresistible. Looking at the pictures, Alan looked through them all. They were all happy, and then there were pictures of the chaos he'd brought down on all of them.

"Me? I want nothing." Alan chuckled.

"Yeah, you want Zero. He fucked up your face, and now it's payback. I always knew Zero had something about him. He wasn't just another pretty face."

Alan landed the first blow to the side of Whizz's face.

He watched as the other man simply spat blood

onto the ground beside him. "You hit like a pussy."

Throwing another blow, Alan gritted his teeth. Whizz groaned but didn't make another move to say anything.

Walking away from the man, he unrolled the torture materials he'd spent the last couple of years training with. The men who collected Whizz were playing cards a couple of feet away. None of them had anything to say to him.

"So, you're friends with Zero."

Whizz laughed. "Zero's a good guy. Everyone is friends with him."

Staring at the pictures, he put a cross through Sophia's face then Nash's. "I'm doing all right taking out the people who mean something to Zero. By the time I'm through with him there will only be a few people standing."

The other man started laughing.

"What the fuck do you have to laugh at?" Alan asked, folding his arms over his chest.

"You've killed a nurse, shot a woman, and stabbed a woman. Every person you've hurt has a fucking cunt. You're nothing but a pussy, and you can't take on a real man." Whizz chuckled. "You've picked off the women. What are you going to do to face the men?"

Alan didn't say anything. He couldn't think of a single comeback to the other man.

"See, you've got nothing."

Picking up the knife, he walked over to Whizz and slammed the blade into his hand going through the wood. Whizz howled in pain, screaming and cursing.

Laughing, he brought another knife toward Whizz, sliding the tip of the blade down his face. "Now, what do you think?" he asked.

"I'm tied to a fucking chair. Try and take me on

when you've got some fucking balls." Whizz spat in Alan's face.

Stepping back, Alan wiped the spittle from his face.

Gripping the knife, he slammed the knife into Whizz's other palm.

Torturing Whizz would give him little satisfaction.

Chapter Thirteen

The drive to the clubhouse was silent. Zero stared out of the window while also holding onto Prue's hand. Nash and Lash had stayed behind at the hospital to keep an eye on their women, not that he could blame him. When Prue was in the hospital, he'd only left at Tiny's orders.

"How is life treating you?" Tiny asked, talking to Devil.

"Can't complain. Club life is amazing. I've got a good woman even though she's having a rough time of it with this latest pregnancy."

He listened to Devil talk about Lexie's rough pregnant state. Glancing at Prue's stomach, he wondered what he would do if anything happened to her.

"Lexie is your wife?" Prue asked.

"Yeah, she's my woman." Devil moved, grabbing out his wallet. "Best thing that happened to me was meeting her. I still can't believe I've settled down for one bitch." He heard the fondness in Devil's voice.

Zero recalled meeting Lexie. She was a tough nut and perfect for Devil.

"That's my son, Simon. There is Judi. She's my daughter, and that there is Elizabeth," Devil said, pointing to all the people in the picture.

"How old is Lexie? She doesn't look old enough to be Judi's mother," Prue asked.

Devil laughed. "Judi is my adoptive daughter. She was being used by a fucking pimp. She's got no other family, but now she's mine. I love her like a daughter."

His respect for Devil went up. "Judi is a sweet girl, quiet at times but sweet. I hope she'll come out of her shell a little. She makes me fucking proud," Devil said.

"Oh, I see."

"Who is staying with them?" Zero asked.

"Ripper and a few of the boys have stayed behind. They won't let any harm come to my women." Devil smiled, turning back to look out of the front.

They pulled into the clubhouse, and there seemed a darkness over the building. The play area was bare, and no one was lingering outside.

"Where is everyone?" he asked, climbing out of the car with difficulty.

"Sophia got attacked while we were all indoors. No one leaves without an escort, and there is a man looking over the security videos."

They were going to ask Whizz to locate the abandoned buildings where there were no owners. Together they walked into the clubhouse. He found Chaos Bleeds sitting nursing beers as he walked in. They were not in the mood to party. He saw the serious expressions on their faces. Curse looked angry.

"How is she?" Curse asked, looking at Tiny then at Devil.

"She's stable. Nash is staying behind," Tiny said.

Zero wrapped his arm around Prue's shoulders watching Tiny go to his woman. Eva was pulled to her feet and kissed with passion. "You're not leaving the clubhouse. You stay here and don't let the kids out, got it?"

"Got it."

"I can't believe you kept me in the dark," Tate said.

Zero saw Tiny's daughter was breaking apart. Her eyes were bloodshot. Tears streaked down her face as she stared at them. "Angel and Sophia are in the hospital. They could die, and you didn't think it was okay to tell me?"

"This is not your club, Tate. Remember your place," Tiny said.

Murphy was trying to console his woman.

"The club? I don't give a fuck about the club. Two women are in the hospital because this fucker couldn't kill someone properly—"

"Enough!" Tiny bellowed the word. Zero held onto Prue as she tensed in his arms and started to shake. "This is my fucking club, and I show you leniency because you're my fucking daughter. Right now, you will keep your mouth shut. I don't need to hear whatever the fuck you've got to say. This is not your club. You're not in control of it. Murphy, keep her quiet, or I'll have her barred from the club after all of this is over." There was silence around the room. Tate kept her mouth shut, sitting down. "Meeting in ten minutes. I want you in my fucking office."

Tiny turned away going into his office and slamming the door.

"Wow, I'm pleased you're not like him, boss. I almost pissed myself," Pussy said, smirking.

Devil whacked Pussy around the back of the head. "Shut the fuck up."

The leader of Chaos Bleeds entered the office.

"Come up to the bedroom with me," Zero said, taking her hand.

She followed him upstairs without causing a fight. He winced at the pain from his wounds. Zero had suffered far worse than the bullet holes. Together they made their way up to the privacy of his bedroom. She closed the door, helping him take the shirt off.

Glancing down at his bound wounds he saw they were not leaking.

"You're going to have to be careful," she said,

touching his body.

"I'll be careful when this fucker is in the ground." He groaned but sat down on the side of his bed. "I wish you were naked and we were about to fuck."

"All you think about is sex," she said, sinking her fingers into his hair.

"When it comes to you all I want to think about is sex." He took her hand and kissed the inside of her wrist. "There's something I want to give you."

"Yeah, I know what you want to give me. You tell me every chance you get."

"It has nothing to do with my hard cock." He chuckled then winced. "Stay here." Getting to his feet he went to the drawer that had all of his toys. Closing the drawer he moved to the top one, pushing his underwear out of the way. Beside his gun lay a small square box. He took it out, walking as best he could back to the bed. She still stood beside his bed, waiting.

"What are you doing?" she asked.

Taking her hand in his, he stared up into her shocking green eyes. "Prue, will you do me the honor of becoming my wife?"

"You're proposing?"

"Yeah, I've got the ring, and I just said the words."

Her gaze went to the ring he held in his palm then to his eyes.

"Are you kidding me?" she asked.

"No, I want you to become my wife."

She pulled away from him, snatching her hand back. "Angel and Sophia are inside the hospital. You've got bullet wounds, and Alan is winning left, right, and center, and you decide to propose to me?"

"I thought this would be a good time to get it out there." He held the box open, shaking it for her to look.

"Have a look. What do you think?"

"You're only proposing because you know you're not going to survive," she said, folding her arms underneath her breasts. "Alan kills us, and you don't have to marry me."

"What world are you on?" he asked. "I'm proposing because I've promised my brother to bring them Alan's head. I've got every intention of surviving." He held up the ring. "Come on, come and have a look. You'll like it, I promise you."

"No," she said, staying where she was.

"What? You can't say no. You've not even seen the ring yet."

"I'm not going to agree to marry you until Alan is gone. Once his threat is gone, ask me again, and I'll see about it."

Zero frowned. His anger spiked. Getting up, he advanced toward her and was pleased that she stepped back going toward the wall.

"This is insane. What are you doing?" she asked.

When he had her trapped against the wall, he rested his arms on either side. He used his body to keep her trapped.

"You're not going to marry me?"

"I didn't say that."

"Marry me," he asked.

"No. Ask me when we're alive and Alan is gone."

Leaning forward, he claimed her lips, slamming his tongue deep into her mouth. She moaned, sinking against him. Her hands wrapped around his body, holding onto him as he took possession of her mouth. "Marry me?"

"Why do you keep asking?"

They were so close. Her breath fanned his face.

"We both know it's what we want. Wear my ring

and become my wife. We're going to survive this. You need to stop being worried about what is not going to happen."

She rested her head against his. Her palm slid down his chest.

"Do you always get what you want?" she asked.

"Most of the time. Wear my ring, and give me what I want." Zero waited for her answer.

"Okay, I'll wear your ring, and after we're done, you better fucking marry me."

Laughing, he retrieved the ring from the box where he'd left it on the bed. He placed the ring on her finger and saw it was a perfect fit.

"We own each other now." Kissing her fingers, he squeezed her hand. "I've got to go to this meeting now."

"I'll help you down."

Together they made their way downstairs. He left her to go into Tiny's office. Most of the men were there, including some men from Chaos Bleeds. The door closed shutting out the rest of the club. The noise diminished, and there was only the silence in the room.

"I want to thank you for coming," Tiny said, looking at Devil.

"I like to think our two clubs are friends, Tiny. You call and I'll come, isn't that right, boys?" Devil asked his crew.

They mumbled their agreements around the room.

Sitting back, Zero rubbed his head feeling the beginnings of a migraine.

"I'm hoping this is the last time you get a call from me. You ever need The Skulls, you just call."

"No offence, but you guys attract trouble. I'd rather not curse my life with you coming to town to help," Devil said, chuckling.

They all had a little laugh at Devil's words.

"Let's get down to business," Tiny said. "Zero believes Alan will be working out of one of the abandoned buildings somewhere." Zero watched as he picked up a file. "Whizz supplied all the information and was going to meet with one of his people to help him figure out a trail Alan took."

Opening the file, Zero checked each one wondering where Alan would settle down to do whatever the fuck he wanted to do.

"Ned has heard of him, but it has been ten years since any news of him has made the rounds through Vegas," Alex said, resting his head against the wall.

"What took you so long finding that shit out?" Butch asked.

"Some people don't like to talk. Lucky for us, Ned is an excellent person in getting the silent to speak."

Zero would bet money the other man was telling the truth. Ned Walker, Eva's father, was a fucking menace.

Tiny's private line started to ring. "What the fuck could it be now?"

He watched Tiny pick up the line. There was silence for several minutes, and it was only Tiny squeezing the receiver that alerted the room to the tension.

"What's going on, Tiny?" Devil asked.

No response came, and then he lowered the phone, pressing a button as it went onto speaker phone.

"I'd like to play a game." Alan's voice came over the line. "Three people get to know one man, and now all three are gone. One fucked him, the other protected, and the other he thought he was in love with. How many women do I have left?"

Gritting his teeth, Zero stared at Tiny, who was

looking at him.

"Zero!" He answered the question while everyone remained silent.

"Ah, the man himself. I take it a couple of bullet holes didn't stop you from leaving the hospital. I thought you'd be by Sophia's side, begging her forgiveness."

He stayed silent, listening as Alan continued to talk.

"Oh, this is so much fun," Alan said, laughing. "Here is another. I'm a computer genius, and I know everything there is to know about everything. Where am I now?"

A loud masculine cry came over the line.

"Whizz."

"Wow, Zero, you surprise me. I didn't think you'd know how to play this game. I'm a little disappointed," Alan said. "Do you hear that? They know who you are."

"Fuck off," Whizz said.

"Nah, I thought about it, but this is too much fun."

"I'm going to fucking kill you and piss on your body when I'm finished." This came from Whizz again.

Glancing at Killer, Zero saw the paleness in the other man's face.

"Do you think I'm scared of dying?" Alan asked. "Newsflash, I'm not scared of dying. In fact, I look forward to the never-ending peace I'll get once I'm dead." Alan sighed over the line. "Now, is the precious Prue there, or have you kept her away from danger?"

"She's not here."

"Then go and get her. I need to speak to the both of you."

Zero was silent. He didn't want her near this fucker. Whizz's wail made Zero get to his feet. When he finally got his hands around Alan's throat, he was going to relish taking his life.

****

Prue couldn't stop staring at the ring on her finger. It was so beautiful, and it took her breath away. The fit was perfect as well. Smiling, she raised her hand up as she stared at it.

"Did Zero propose to you?" Tate asked, sitting beside her.

She was sitting in the pantry surrounded by food. It was the only area in the clubhouse that was silent from all the chaos that was happening. The other woman looked a mess. She sniffled, wiping her eyes with a tissue.

"Yes, he proposed." She pushed her glasses up her nose to glance at the other woman.

"He'll make a good husband one day." Tate's lips were quivering.

They were never going to be great friends, but Prue avoided fights whenever she could. "Are you all right?"

"Yeah, I'm fine. I put Simon to bed. Murphy is in with my father. I just want some peace," Tate said.

"What if your boy wakes up?"

Tate produced a baby monitor. "He usually screams for me or his dad." She shrugged. "I just need a few minutes. I don't know how long that meeting's going to go, and I want a few minutes away from Murphy."

Sitting in the pantry, Prue stared at the array of spices opposite her. She turned the ring on her finger, sliding it on, then off.

"I'm not a total bitch. At least, I wasn't always a total bitch," Tate said. "I love my friends, and I love my family. There are times I just hate the club, but then there are times I love the club. Fuck, I'm messed up in the head." Tate ran fingers through her hair. "Angel is my best friend. Kelsey is as well. Angel has been there a lot longer."

"Look, you really don't need to say anything to me," Prue said, holding her hands up.

"I know. We're not friends. We'll never be friends, but we'll make do because of our men and the club. I just need to talk to someone who won't rub my back and make me feel all right. You're not like that." Tate turned to her. "I don't like being kept in the dark. My friends are in danger, and I can't handle not knowing."

"What do you want from me?" Prue asked.

"This man, will he get worse?"

Opening her lips, she thought about it. Frowning, Prue shook her head. "I don't know him. Until this shit started I didn't even know who he was."

"He doesn't care about anything, does he?"

Prue shook her head. "You need to take care. He'll kill or hurt whoever is close to Zero."

Tate nodded. "We don't have to talk now. Can I just sit here for a while?"

"This is your club not mine."

"You marry Zero and you'll inherit it. The club is the life."

Prue didn't argue with the other woman. Rubbing her hands down her legs she rested her head against the wall trying to imagine her life with Zero. She smiled at the thought of him picking her up from school. The kids would want to know everything about the man with the bike.

Running fingers through her hair she let out a sigh.

Becoming Zero's woman would be a dream come true. She only wished that Trevor was here to see them be together. Her brother would be pissed, but he would also be happy for them. She'd make sure of it.

"Prue." Zero's yell invaded her calm and serene moment.

"I'm being called," she said. Turning to Tate she saw the tears falling thick and fast. "Don't let it get to you. Your son needs his mother to be strong. Ignore Alan. You mean nothing to Zero and will be safe." She tapped her leg then made her way out of the pantry.

Zero was passing as she did. "Hey," she said, grabbing his attention.

"Where were you?" he asked, cupping her cheek. He looked panicked.

"I was having a few moments to myself. What's going on? What's the matter?"

He took her hand leading her back toward the office. "Alan's got Whizz. He's torturing him and wanted you with us when we talk."

Zero no longer had to pull on her arm. She followed him straight to Tiny's office. The men were tense as screams filled the room. Alan was pushing the men too far.

"Fucking stop it," Zero said. "I've got her with me."

The screaming stopped. "Prue, honey, are you there?" Alan asked. The way he spoke made it sound like they had some kind of connection.

"Yeah, I'm here."

"That wasn't loud enough. Do a bit better than that."

"I'm here." She yelled the words, hating him more.

Whizz screamed once again as Alan laughed. She couldn't handle the sound and shouted for him to stop.

"Stop it, fucking stop it. I'm here. Hurting him is

not going to achieve anything. You want us to know you've got the balls to hurt someone, fine, we know. You've hurt him, and we know you've got the balls to do it," she said.

Zero held her hand tightly. She felt all their gazes on her as she spoke.

"So the silent sister does speak."

"Trevor never spoke for me. I wouldn't have let him come near you if I knew what you had planned." Prue folded her arms, feeling stupid for being angry at the phone.

"I know. He talked about you often, how clever you were. I always wondered how a primary teacher could be clever. Now, I don't care," Alan said.

"You're growing bored." Prue was shaking inside, hoping her gut was right.

"Why would you say that?"

Looking toward Zero, he nodded letting her continue. "You've waited ten years for revenge. In the hospital you told me you had to wait to fix everything Zero broke. It took you years to get to the condition you are in now." She closed her eyes focusing on Alan rather than the men wanting to kill the man. "Within twenty-four hours you've shot one woman, stabbed another, and Zero also has two bullet wounds in his body. You're getting bored with waiting."

"I've got Whizz to keep me company."

Another scream rent the air.

"He's not who you want," Prue said, forcing herself to speak up.

"Go on."

"If you wanted Whizz this would be it and you'd be gone. You want me and Zero. Trevor is gone. One down, two to go. I'm not dead. You can't get over your revenge until we are both dead."

"I'm hurting Zero."

"Really? How are you hurting him?" she asked.

"Angel is the sweet one of the club. Everyone loves her. He fancied himself in love with Sophia. I've got what I want."

"No, you haven't. You're wrong on both counts." She twirled the ring she wore around her finger.

Opening her eyes, she pressed a finger to her lips signaling for the men to be silent. She was surprised they were giving her this moment to talk with him. Prue was gambling with a guess. Alan had only talked to her twice, and his sudden backlash was desperate. She was losing interest as well. Prue wanted to marry Zero and get Alan out of their lives forever.

"Why am I wrong?" Alan asked. She had his attention, which was good to know.

"Zero hates Angel." Prue stared at Zero, letting him know she was bluffing. "He told me she was a pain in the ass. Her presence was a thorn in his side. Always needing protecting, always crying. Let me tell you, Alan, I know Zero, he can't stand someone who moans and cries all the time. It gets a little boring."

When they were growing up, Prue had gotten her and Trevor out of a lot of trouble with her ability to make up tales.

"Really?"

"Yes, the only person he cares about is Lash. Having Angel out of the way would make life so much easier."

"What about Sophia?" Alan asked.

Was he buying the lies?

"She was a slut. Zero told me he had to practically peel the woman off him. The moment Nash was out of the room she was driving him crazy with her insatiable appetite."

Prue shrugged her shoulders at Zero.

Give me a break. I'm making this shit up out of my own head.

"Also, he proposed to me. Zero always comes back to me," she said, smiling. This part was not a lie. "Whizz is not Zero's friend either. He belongs to The Skulls."

"Well, I guess we both have a problem," Alan said.

"No, you don't." She reached out, grabbing Zero's hand.

"No?" Alan asked.

"We'll make a trade. Zero and myself for Whizz."

Zero shook his head. "No, Alan. I'll trade Whizz's life for myself. Leave her out of it."

"Nah, I like the way your woman works. She knows her stuff."

Silence was on the other end. "I'll get my men to dump Whizz somewhere. I want you to meet me. You'll come alone or else."

"What will you do if we don't?" Prue said, feeling Zero's anger directed at her.

"I've got ways. You don't come alone, Angel and Sophia will get a healthy dose of poison injected into their veins. I'm not so fucking stupid, but I think it's time for us to get to the end of this game. I expect you where this all began. You know the location of where Trevor took his last breath. I think it's only fair we end it there."

Alan hung up. There was silence over the line.

"You're so fucking stupid," Zero said, releasing his anger on her.

She touched his hands. Tears filled her eyes at the blatant anger directed at her.

"Why the fuck did you do that? He doesn't need

to have you."

"He's right, Prue. That was fucking stupid," Tiny said.

"This is a game to him. One down, two to go. He takes you, then he's after me anyway."

"I wouldn't let that happen. Ten years ago I was a young fucking fool. I'm not a fool anymore. I wouldn't let any harm come to you."

She smiled. "It wouldn't matter. Alan wouldn't have agreed until he got what he wanted, which is both of us there."

Zero shook his head. "I'm so fucking angry at you right now."

"Save the anger. I get that she lied, but now you've got a big fucking problem," Devil said, moving away from the wall.

"What problem is that?" Zero asked.

"Alan is expecting you both to be there alone. I'm a betting man, and I've got a feeling he will find a way to put poison into Angel and Sophia. How the fuck are you two going to get out of that shit?" Devil asked.

Glancing at Zero, he shrugged.

"There is no plan," Zero said.

"No, you can't do that," Tiny said. "There has to be some kind of plan."

"There is. Get Whizz out alive, kill the bastard, and let Nash and Lash know there is someone walking around the hospital. They deserve some justice. Prue and I will make do and take Alan out." Zero looked at her.

She trusted him with her whole heart. Tears filled her eyes knowing this could be her last day on earth. There is no one else she would want to spend it with than with Zero. Smiling at him, she tugged him down to kiss his lips. "Come on, let's go and face the music."

Ten years they'd been apart, and now in some

sick twist of fate, Alan had brought them back together. Holding Zero's hand, she made her way out of the room and toward Alan.

Chapter Fourteen

"You're going to let them do this alone?" Devil asked.

Tiny turned to look at his men and then at his friend. "This is what Zero wants. We've got to get Whizz and then to the hospital." He lifted the phone and made the call to the two of his men. Once he told the two brothers about the danger he hung up.

He was torn in two over what to do. In all of his life he'd never left anyone behind. Zero had proven time and time again his loyalty was to The Skulls.

"I'm not letting them do anything alone. Do you think I like the thought of my men and their women hurting? It fucking kills me inside." Tiny slammed a palm to his chest. "Just once I'd like to get by in peace, but we've all got a fucking past, and it always comes to bite us in the ass one way or another."

"Get the fuck out," Devil said, looking around the room.

Tiny gave a nod of his head for his men to leave.

"You can't leave them alone." Devil faced him with his arms folded.

"We're not going to leave them alone. We can't exactly go following them on our bikes either."

The far door opened. Tiny had left his cell phone on for Eva to hear the whole conversation. There were tears in her eyes, and she held a set of keys out toward the men.

"I know where they're going," she said. "I'm tagging along. I know the road quite well."

His heart gave out. Eva was a strong woman. She matched him in all things.

"Baby, I can't let you drive us out. He's a lunatic."

"So? I grew up with lunatics, and I'm no stranger to a man's anger. I will not stand idly by while Zero and Prue die because of this fucker." Eva held the keys to her heart. "You're taking me, or you're not going anywhere."

Walking forward, Tiny watched her take a step back. "Baby, go and get in the fucking car. We've got a man to fuck up."

****

"You don't have to do this," Zero said, glancing over at his woman.

They were sat in the car about to pull out of the lot.

"I have to do this. He killed Trevor. I'm not going to let him take this from us." She was rubbing her temple, staring straight out of the window. He caught sight of the diamond ring on her finger. When all of this was over he was going to marry this woman and claim her for his own.

"That doesn't mean you've got to stay with me," he said. "This is not your fight. I hurt this man, tortured him. He's coming for me."

She shook her head. "We're in this together."

Taking her hand, he pulled out of the compound seeing his men, The Skulls, watching them all go. Butch was there at the end. Zero bit his lip seeing his friend watching them leave.

"We'll get through this. It's going to be fun."

He chuckled. "You're the first woman I know who will find this coming fight fun."

"I've never been in a true fight before. This is going to be hardcore." He felt her hand tremble within his.

"Where do you want to go for our honeymoon?" Zero asked, changing the subject.

"Really? You want to talk about that now?"

"Why not? We're going to have that conversation anyway, so why not now?"

He worked his way out of the town, watching everyone pass as if nothing had happened.

"I'd like to go somewhere hot," she said. "How about the Caribbean?"

"Nah, I don't want the Caribbean. I want somewhere cold so you've got no choice but to wrap up warm with me."

"If it's warm we can be naked without fear of dying," she said. "I'll even wear a bikini for you."

Zero groaned. The thought of seeing Prue in a skimpy swimming set was too much. His cock thickened, and all he wanted to do was drive them to the nearest airport and take her away.

"We're going to the Caribbean, and you'll wear a lovely bikini, which I can take off with my teeth," he said.

She giggled. "You're insatiable."

"I know, but it's all directed at you."

They talked for the first fifteen minutes of the drive about their wedding. He knew his brothers wouldn't accept being in suits for the wedding. Prue didn't want them in suits. She wanted the men to wear their leathers as she walked down the aisle in a white wedding dress.

"The boys are going to love you," he said, laughing.

"It's what I want. We'll pay the church the proper money for us to get what we want."

"Okay, I'm game if you are," he said. "Tiny will help pay for the wedding, or at least the club will."

For several minutes they were silent. Zero recognized the road. He'd not been down this road for a long time. Memories of Trevor dying in his arms were too much.

"Where are we going?"

"Trevor stayed in a hotel room when he called me. He was bleeding out and knew they'd come to finish him off in a hospital. Before he died he wanted to talk to me about you. He asked for me to keep you safe." He laughed. The sound was hollow. "How fucking safe am I keeping you when I'm leading you to the man who killed your brother?"

She squeezed his hand. "Don't let that happen. What happened afterward?"

"I burned the building to the ground. No one else was inside the hotel either. Only the person on reception who was too late in calling for help, so the whole building burned to the ground. Since then it was demolished, rebuilt, and is now an abandoned factory. The economy really hit the factories hard. A lot of places closed down, and not all of them have been rebuilt." He rubbed at his temple.

"Why is he doing this?"

"He wants us on edge. This is where Trevor died in my arms. He's going to test us by throwing everything at us." Zero shrugged. "We're strong together, baby. We'll get through this."

"I love you," she said.

"I love you, too."

They were silent as the building came into view. It was such a horrid vision, and he couldn't help but imagine Trevor placing a hand on his shoulder.

You can do this.

Parking the car, he climbed out staring at the building. Rubbing his eyes, he tried to clear his vision. Staring at the factory he saw several windows were smashed, and the whole building itself looked like it was crumbling. Graffiti coated the walls with names or pictures. One picture was of a cock with large balls.

Shaking his head, he looked down at the floor. Prue grabbed his hand. "We can do this. We're in this together. We've always been in this together."

Feeling her strength, he took several steps forward. He paused when he saw a man wearing a hood walk out of the building.

"Well, well, well, I really thought I'd have to send a message to my men," Alan said, raising the cell phone to his ear. "Back off. He's here, and he's here alone."

He watched Alan throw away the cell phone.

"Are you going to stay hidden behind that hood?" Zero asked.

"I guess now is a good time as any." Alan removed the hood.

Zero didn't make any move, but the man's face was a complete mess. Ten years ago he hadn't shown any kind of mercy. There were also burn marks over his face. The picture Whizz had gotten hadn't done the man justice.

"I'm a fucking beauty, don't you think?" Alan asked. His gaze turned to Prue. She didn't look shocked or even scared. "Would you fuck me, baby?"

"No, you killed my brother."

"The only reason?"

"No. You fucking repulse me, and it has nothing to do with the scars. Your *game* is what turns me off."

Alan looked up at the sky and started laughing. "Ah, I really do love my games. It was a stroke of genius. Seeing men, hard-nosed men, turn into a bunch of fucking pussies. It was brilliant."

Zero gripped Prue's hand tighter. He was really struggling to keep his anger at bay. Those men were his friends. They had been through so much, and the women didn't deserve that kind of pain.

"The whore nurse you fucked was especially delightful. She squealed like a little bitch with every cut I made."

"So did you if I remember correctly."

Alan's smile vanished, and his face turned into thunderous rage.

"Where is Whizz?" Zero asked.

"Now, the computer nerd was a delight. He's never going to be the same after I got through with him."

He watched Alan grab his cock giving it a rub.

Zero's stomach turned. He hoped to God Alan didn't rape Whizz. He was sick to his stomach, his rage simmering, waiting to be released.

"Call your bastards. I'm sure they're there."

Pulling out his cell phone he dialed Tiny's number.

"Hello," Butch said, answering.

"Butch, where's Tiny?"

"You don't need to know that now. We've got Whizz. He's in a fucking awful state. The bastard, he, erm—fuck, I'm not telling you. I've got to get him to the hospital. Get that fucker to hurt," Butch said.

"The person with him?"

"Dead. We let him tell Alan that he was alive and well. This fucker won't be doing any more damage. Before your call Lash phoned. They've taken out the two men who were going to kill their women. Alan gave the order to kill. The fucker was lying the whole time. He was going to kill them all." Butch explained everything. Prue kept her gaze on Alan, and he held her hand.

"Take care," Zero said.

"You listen to me, Lucas Blakely. You're my best friend, and I will not be held responsible for your death. You will beat this bastard and come home to all us."

"I will. I've got my woman at my side."

"Don't do anything stupid," Butch said.

Hanging up the phone, he placed it back in his pocket.

"Is everything okay?" Prue asked.

"Yes."

Alan started laughing, and their gazes landed back on him. "Now, I've given you back Whizz, and I've got the two of you. I think it's time for us all to play a game."

"I'm a bit old for games," Zero said.

"No one is ever too old for games, especially not the games I play," Alan took a step closer until only a few feet divided them.

The scars on Alan's face didn't fill Zero with happiness. This fucker in a matter of weeks and days had hurt his club.

Alan withdrew a gun. Zero tugged Prue behind him.

"Now, my game is going to be fun," he said. "No, you don't get to hide that bitch. She has to play her part."

Prue stepped from behind him and stood by his side with her head held high.

"She looks so fucking sexy. I see why you're going to marry her," Alan said. "I bet her ass would be a fucking dream to sink into."

Zero stared at the other man, wishing he would shut the fuck up.

A second gun was produced, and he held it up in the air. "Now, I've not thought of a name for this game. It's going to be fun. Do you want to know the rules?"

****

Prue stared at both guns, wondering what the hell they were going to do. Zero wasn't even shaking as he stared at the man opposite them. She wanted to run away and never look back. Staying by Zero's side would win the battle. Tightening her grip in his hand, she waited for Alan to tell them about the game.

"Now, it took me a little while to think about this game, so bear with me." He raised the gun, and Prue ducked instinctively.

Alan laughed, mocking her movements.

She really wanted this bastard to die and to die now.

"Tell us about the fucking game," Zero said.

"It's quite simple. For every bullet I put inside you, she gets to have a shot at me."

Eyes widening, she looked at Zero. Didn't Alan know she could shoot and shoot well?

Zero gave her a quick squeeze. She wanted to jump with joy but knew they had to keep their wits about them. If she started acting all excited then Alan would change the game.

"If she shoots you?" Zero asked.

"I doubt that's going to happen." Alan showed them the gun was loaded and got it ready. He aimed for the building and fired the first bullet. A window shattered in the background. "I don't cheat," Alan said. "I shoot you, and she gets a chance to shoot me."

This has to be some kind of mistake.

"What are you thinking?" Alan asked.

"Why are you trusting her with a gun?"

Alan laughed. "Trevor talked all the time about the pair of you. I recall him saying how you and he would train for hours shooting a gun. Not once did he mention her involvement. She doesn't own a gun of her own. I checked. This is going to be a fun game. Your life is in her hands."

The gun she owned wasn't registered. It had been given to her by Zero a long time ago, and she kept it in top condition. He'd also bought her the ammo to be able to use it.

Trevor and Zero wouldn't tell their parents that they were teaching her. She did own a gun, but she kept it hidden inside her home.

"All I've got to do is shoot you?" Prue asked, trying to appear scared.

"Yes."

He gave the gun a spin and offered it up to her.

Withdrawing her hand from Zero's she took several steps closer to Alan. Taking the gun from him she felt the calm settle over her at the feel of the gun in her hands. This was going to be easy.

"Now, step away from him," Alan said.

She took several steps away from Zero. His gaze was on her, and she recognized it from when she was younger.

"Keep the target in sight, shoot straight, and never take your eye off the target."

He'd held her hand steady, aimed, and they'd fired at the cans or bottles they found.

"You look kind of sexy with that gun. Maybe I'll chain you up and fuck you while you're holding it," Alan said.

Her stomach roiled, sickened by the vision he created.

There was no way she was letting this man touch her.

How are you going to watch him take a shot at Zero?

Closing her eyes, she tried to think of something else. Putting her feelings aside was never going to be an option.

When she opened her eyes she saw Alan was focused on Zero once again.

"Are we ready to play this game?" Alan asked.

Looking at Zero, she saw he was looking at her. His eyes seemed to say a million words.

The sound of a bullet rang out, and Zero collapsed to the ground. Staring in shock, she saw his leg was bleeding. Alan had shot him in the leg.

Without thinking, she pointed the gun and stared at Alan. She'd never killed a man before.

"Go on, little girl. Show me what you've got, if you can. He's going to die."

"Target," Zero said. "Imagine a can."

His words invaded her thoughts. She looked at Alan down the barrel.

"Keep the target in sight, shoot straight, and never take your eye off the target," Zero said, speaking the words once again.

"What?" Alan asked.

She shot the first bullet, and it hit Alan in the leg. Stepping forward, she brought her hand up to hold the gun securely as she fired a second shot taking out his other leg. Alan squealed in pain.

In her mind she saw her brother. He had been too young to die. Then she saw the nurse. Even though the blonde had fucked Zero, she didn't deserve to die. Next she saw Angel, Sophia, Lash, and Nash. None of them deserved this, and she approached the fucker who was the cause of so much pain and misery.

The shock in his eyes was easy.

"What?" he asked again, gasping.

"I was a better shot than my brother."

The gun in Alan's hand started to rise, and she shot another bullet into his arm before putting a second bullet in his other.

Pain, anger, rage, took over. She couldn't focus on anything but the need for vengeance on this man who had taken so much from her.

Alan screamed in pain, but it still wasn't enough. Stamping on his balls, she watched him howl but not be able to do anything. Tears ran down her cheeks, and she kept hurting the man in front of her. He had taken everything, and now it was her turn to hurt him. Stepping away, she shot a bullet to his cock then to his stomach.

Finally, she aimed at his head and fired. She kept on firing until the bullets stopped coming. When that wasn't enough, she grabbed the gun on the ground and used that to finish the man off until he was nothing more than a mess on the stones.

She was sobbing when arms came around her.

"You've got him, Prue, he's dead." Tiny held her tight, and she dropped the gun. The tears she thought she'd cried many times finally came back. Staring at the mess, she was pleased to know he wouldn't be coming back.

"He hasn't got a head," she said, after some minutes past.

"What?" Devil asked, looking impressed as he stared down at the body.

"Zero promised to send Lash and Nash this bastard's head," Prue said.

She turned to see Zero hopping toward them. Devil helped hold onto him, giving him some dignity in his walk.

"We've got Tiny's and Devil's voices. This bastard is not coming back," Zero said. When he opened his arms, she went toward him without thinking.

"Remind me to never get on your bad side, babe," Devil said. "This fucker is a fucking mess."

Tucking her head against Zero's chest, she held on tightly to him, never wanting to let go. "We need to get you to the hospital."

"Fuck, Eva's going to be pissed. He's going to bleed all over the back seats," Tiny said.

The sound of another car arriving drew their attention. Alex and several of Devil's men climbed out. "We needed for the cleanup?"

"Yeah, he's there," Tiny said.

She followed the two men toward their car, which was hidden around the other side of the building. Alan had been too busy concentrating on them to hear the car approach.

Zero held onto her as they made their way into the car. She tried to keep his leg off the fabric as Tiny drove toward the hospital.

The doctors and nurses took Zero away to deal with the wound. She followed Tiny and Devil down toward Lash and Nash.

Tiny made her tell each man what she did. Their arms going around her would stay with her forever.

"You're one of us now," Lash said. "The club will protect you always."

"I'm going to marry Zero," she said.

"Even without being his old lady, you'd still be one of the club and under our protection."

She smiled and followed Tiny toward Whizz's room.

Walking into the room, she held back a gasp at the mess before her. His hands and feet were covered in bandages. His face was also covered, and he was hooked up to several machines.

"Hey," Tiny said, approaching the bed. "How are you doing?"

"I'm dancing for joy," Whizz said.

His gaze fell on her. Going to him, she placed a hand gently against his face. She would never turn away from this man. "I killed him," she said.

"What?"

"I shot his head right off, and I made him hurt for several minutes." She licked her lips, staring into his eyes. "I know it doesn't give you anything, but I promise you, Whizz, he hurt before he died."

"Thank you."

"I'll come and visit you soon."

She left the bedroom giving Tiny time with the other man. Sitting in the reception she waited for the doctor to tell her about Zero's progress. A couple of hours later she was being led into another private room. He was sitting up in bed.

When he opened his arms she went to him, climbing up on the bed to hold him.

"Do I repulse you now?" she asked.

"You make me proud. I knew you'd take him out. I trusted you to do it. He killed your brother and hurt people. I'm not repulsed by you. You're going to be my wife."

She smiled, resting her head against his chest.

"Don't leave me," she said.

"Baby, you're going to be begging for some privacy."

Smiling, she didn't move from that position, holding onto him to give her the warmth she needed.

Chapter Fifteen

Five months later

Zero looked out of the summer house to see Prue walking across the clear beach with the blue ocean at her back. They were married and finally on their honeymoon after the chaos Alan had put them through. Zero circled the ring on his finger, feeling complete for once in his life. With Alan's presence in their life, the club had suffered in ways he didn't want to think about on this time with his wife.

Whizz wasn't the same. He left hospital one month after the attack and had Sandy deal with his wounds. Where Zero had put a blade in Alan's back, the other man had come up with another way of torturing Whizz. Now the other man never left the club without a weapon. He didn't drink, and he wouldn't be around new people who visited the club. He had moved in with Killer and Kelsey, not being able to handle club life.

One night before Whizz had moved out, Zero had woken up to hear terrified screams. He and Prue had gone to Whizz's room and it took them a long time to bring him out of the nightmare. Throughout the night, Zero offered to watch over him while Prue held him in her arms, trying to send the demons away. He wasn't jealous of the other man. Nothing about Whizz was sexual.

Killer had even told him that Whizz would share his and Kelsey's bed if the nights got too hard. It wasn't about sex. They were all simply caring for the man who had been taken and tortured.

Sophia had made it out of the hospital in one piece. Nothing was damaged with her, but she was scared. The baby had been lost during the attack, but the doctors said she was fine for other children. She had begged Nash and all of the men to teach her self-defense. All of the women requested it. With Prue's help, they were able to take care of themselves. To make sure they could handle themselves Nash had recreated that night where Sophia was stabbed. They were all present as Nash attacked Sophia from behind and she took him out with her fists. They had applauded her strength, and Nash spent the rest of the night comforting a teary-eyed woman. None of the women were going to be victims again.

Zero stared down at the photo Lash had sent. Angel had woken up from her coma three days after Whizz was admitted. She had remembered everything that happened and had the use of her legs. The doctors had been concerned about her legs with the bullet lodging close to her spine.

She made a full recovery with the club supporting her every step of the way. The innocent young woman had earned all of their respect. She had stood in front of a bullet and almost died for them. Lash stayed for Zero's wedding at Angel's request, but now he was in Italy enjoying a much needed vacation.

The picture on Zero's phone was of Angel, their son, and Lash, wrapping his arms around all of them.

In some way they had all survived. When he got out of the hospital together Prue and Zero had visited Trevor's graveside. He had held a sobbing Prue as she poured out her confession of killing Alan.

Putting the cell phone down, he made his way out toward his wife. She was looking out at the ocean. Tiny had paid for them to go away to the Caribbean. The club adored Prue. She was a strong woman, and they respected that.

Wrapping his arms around her waist, he pulled

her close. "What are you thinking about?"

"Our wedding. It really was beautiful."

True to her word, Prue had asked the men to wear their leathers and Tiny had given her away. Zero would always remember her walking down to become his wife.

"Do you believe I love you now?" he asked.

"Yes, there's nothing like putting your life in my hands for me to believe you," she said, smiling.

"I want to fuck you," he said.

"Then lead me to our room and fuck me, husband."

Taking hold of her hand, he led her back into the house. Picking her up, he carried her upstairs to their bedroom. Dropping her onto the bed, he removed the bikini she wore with his teeth. He stared down at her creamy pussy feeling an answering need inside him.

Tearing off his shorts, he gripped his shaft running the tip through her slit. Her cream coated his shaft, and he plunged inside her warmth, feeling her moan around his cock.

"Please," she said.

"Take all of my cock, baby." He thrust inside her, over and over again. Zero loved the feel of her tight warmth around his cock. "When I fuck your pussy and fill you with my cum I'm going to take your ass."

"Yes, please, Zero, fuck my pussy and then my ass."

Gripping her hips, he pounded inside her pussy, relishing each pleasured cry as he took her to the edge of bliss. Zero refused to let her go over the edge into pleasure. He held her tightly, taking possession of her lips like he'd done so many times before.

"I want to hear you scream my name," he said, slamming into her slowly, making her take every inch of his thick cock.

"Please, stop torturing me," she said, whimpering.

Kissing down her body, he flicked a nipple, sucking the hard bud into his mouth.

"Fuck, I love your tits," he said.

Staring down at where they were joined he watched his slick prick slide in then out of her body. It was so erotic, and he couldn't look away.

"So pretty," he said.

"What is?"

"Your red pussy taking my cock is a thing of beauty. I'm never going to get bored with watching you take me."

He growled out the words. Leaning down, he sucked onto her neck, moaning as the pleasure was too much.

Pounding inside her, he cried out as with one final plunge he shot his cum deep into her womb. Zero dug his fingers into her hips, knowing he would leave bruises on her skin.

"Fuck, baby, I love you," he said, plunging his tongue into her mouth.

She ran her fingers up and down his chest.

"I'm never going to get enough of you and that hard cock."

Zero smiled down at her. He made to pull out, but she held him tightly inside her.

"No, don't go yet. What's the rush?"

"I want inside your ass."

"Stop being greedy. You've already claimed my pussy."

"I always want more."

Lying down beside her, he stayed within her warmth and stroked her body. She shook underneath him. Each quiver seemed to make her pussy clench around his shaft.

"This is amazing," she said, looking up at him.

"What is?"

"This, our being together. I know Trevor would be happy."

He brushed his lips against hers. "I know he will."

Prue had sold her house and had moved in with him. She hadn't started looking for work at the schools, which he was pleased about. Zero liked to keep her by his side at all times.

"How did you know I wouldn't miss?" she asked.

"You're a great shot. I also knew you loved me, Prue. After that one bullet you wouldn't let him win. The moment Alan put a bullet in me, he'd cemented his fate." Touching her lips, he felt his cock thicken once again.

"You're insatiable."

"Only for you." He kissed her head, grabbing her hand to place over his heart. "I'm all for you."

In front of Prue he had apologized to Sophia and Nash about his behavior. He really was in love with Prue and had been for a long time. It was his own pain and stubbornness that had kept him away from her.

****

Pulling off his cock, Prue moved to the bathroom and grabbed a tube of lubricant she had seen him hide there on their first night inside the house. Entering the bedroom, she held it up for him to see.

"Do you want to play?" she asked, smiling.

"More than you realize."

He climbed off the bed, wrapping his arms around her waist. Zero picked her up and carried her across the room to lie on the bed.

She giggled as he caressed up her body, stroking every inch of her.

"Stop, please, you're tickling me."

Zero placed her on her hands and knees before him. She moaned as his fingers entered her pussy, stroking through her slit to touch her clit. Moving on his stroking fingers, she moaned at the pleasure that consumed her from his touch alone. She was on fire, burning for the need to feel his cock inside her.

"Fuck, you're so fucking hot."

"Fuck me, Zero. Fuck my ass and make it yours," she said.

Looking over her shoulder, she watched him open the tube of lubricant and smear a good amount over his cock before putting some on his fingers and turning back to her.

"I'm not going to go easy on you, baby."

"I don't care. Give me everything you've got," she said, wanting his cock inside her ass. He'd been playing with her ass using his fingers or the dildos he loved to buy. Each time he played with her, she was practically begging for him to finally fuck her hard.

He wouldn't do it and made her take what he gave her.

It was deeply unfair, but at least now he was giving her what she wanted.

Cool fingers pressed to her asshole while his other fingers stroked her clit.

"Come on, baby, give me that orgasm I know you want so badly."

Groaning, she closed her eyes as pleasures mixed together. His touch drove her crazy. Two fingers pressed to her ass, stretching her open. She groaned as he pressed them slowly inside her.

"I've got to get you ready so you can take all of my cock. I'm not a small man," he said, biting her ass.

She yelped at the feel of his teeth against her.

"Don't bite my ass."

He bit her again to let her know who was boss. "You'll take what I'm going to give you, and you're not going to complain either."

Zero's bossiness turned her on. Smiling against the sheet, she moaned as he stretched her ass. Her orgasm was close. She felt her body tighten as his fingers glided through her slit. "Please," she said, begging. "I need to feel you inside me."

Smiling, she felt his fingers withdraw from her ass, but he kept stroking her clit. "You're going to come on my fingers before I fuck your ass."

Groaning in frustration, she rode his fingers begging for him to fuck her. Zero was stubborn and kept touching her pussy until she crashed into orgasm. Screaming out her pleasure, she didn't want it to end, and then it was too much for her.

"Please, stop, fuck me."

His fingers left her slit, and she felt the tip of his cock pressing to her ass. Prue tensed up, and it took time for her to relax.

Zero soothed her, caressing the base of her back as he pushed the head of his cock past the tight ring of muscles keeping him out. "That's it, baby. Take my cock in your hot ass."

Inch by glorious inch, Zero slid his cock into her ass, and Prue took him. She loved the feel of being filled. Her body was on fire, and she wanted to finally have him possess every inch of her.

He gripped her hips and slammed inside her the last inch.

Together they groaned, the sounds echoing off the walls. Tightening her fists in the bed sheet, she waited for the bite of pain to ease slightly.

"You're so fucking hot, baby. Fuck me, I'm

going to be spending a lot of fucking time in this hot fucking ass."

Smiling, she wriggled her ass and Zero proceeded to smack her. "Stay the fuck still."

Wriggling again, she groaned as he spanked her ass to keep her still. Nothing was keeping her still when all she wanted to do was move.

After several minutes of him spanking each of her ass cheeks, Zero finally moved within her ass. He pulled out until only the tip remained inside.

When he plunged back, she screamed at the pain and pleasure.

"Fuck, if I hurt you tell me. I want you to love this, not hate it."

"I do love it. Please, don't stop."

She groaned, thrusting back against his hard cock.

Zero didn't let up. He fucked her ass, gripping her hips hard as he pounded away inside her. She screamed, cried, and finally started to stroke her clit at the pleasure. Prue needed to come, and he ordered her to play.

Within minutes she found her second orgasm as Zero thrust inside her one final time. They came together. Their moans came together, and Zero collapsed over her as his cock jerked deep inside her, filling her with his cum.

"Fuck, how the fuck am I going to survive you?" he asked.

"I don't know. We can die together," she said.

Before she could protest, he picked her up, carrying her through to the bathroom. In the shower he kissed her deeply making her moan with each touch and caress.

After he cleaned her body, removing all trace of their lovemaking, he carried her back to their bed where he laid her down.

For the rest of the night he kissed and stroked her body, loving every inch of her. "Your curves are my new favorite toy," he said, dropping kisses to her lips. "I own every inch of you now," he said, smiling down at her.

"And I own every inch of you."

"I owe you my life, baby. Not only did you save me from a murderous bastard, you gave me a reason to live."

She smiled, touching his check. "A debt of life. You're going to have a horrid life. The only way I want you to pay me back is by spending the rest of your days with me."

"Baby, I got the better end of the deal. It's the best debt I'm ever going to repay."

He claimed her lips, moving her ready to claim her once again. Prue was on cloud nine. She had Zero's love, and she couldn't think of anything better to have in the world.

Epilogue

Butch had thought long and hard about what he was going to do. If he wanted Cheryl and the chance to be with her son, then he was going to have to make sacrifices. Glancing around the club, he saw Whizz was in the corner drinking a coffee. He looked troubled, with Killer and a heavily pregnant Kelsey watching him.

Tate and Murphy were sitting, talking.

It was a Friday night, and he didn't want to be here anymore. Cheryl was his future. Nothing had happened between them. Whenever he went to visit her either at the church or at home, she offered him a hot chocolate and conversation. She was the first woman to not demand anything other than a chat.

Not once had she showed off her body or flashed her tits.

Getting up from his seat he made his way toward Tiny's office. He heard the groans coming from inside.

Knocking, he knew he was going to get fucked, but he needed to do this. It was do this or live with regret.

"This better be fucking good," Tiny said. "Come in."

Opening the door, he saw Eva was staring out of the window. Her clothes were all over the place.

"Butch, what can I do for you?" Tiny asked.

"There's something I need to talk with you about." Butch stood opposite the desk.

"What can I do for you?"

He removed his jacket, the leather cut of The Skulls, and placed it on the desk. "I'm out."

"What?"

"There is a woman I want, and I know I can't go to her until I know for certain this life is behind me."

Tiny was silent, staring at him, and Eva had even

turned to look at him.

"With everything that has happened I will not risk her life. I'm out."

"You're quitting The Skulls for a woman?" Tiny asked.

"Yes." Butch stared at his cut, missing the feel of it on his body. "My stuff is already packed, and I'm leaving."

He got up from his chair, shook Tiny's hand and headed toward the door. His time with The Skulls was over.

The End

SAM CRESCENT

EVERNIGHT PUBLISHING ®

www.evernightpublishing.com

CPSIA information can be obtained
at www.ICGtesting.com
Printed in the USA
LVHW040055190419
614781LV00001B/23